GHOSTS OF THE PAST

MATTHEW LEDREW

GHOSTS OF THE PAST

CORAL BEACH CASEFILES

Published in Canada by Engen Books, St. John's, NL.

Library and Archives Canada Cataloguing in Publication
LeDrew, Matthew, 1984-, author
        Ghosts of the past / Matthew LeDrew.
(Black womb ; 5)
Originally published: St. John's, NL : Engen Books, 2010.
ISBN 978-1-926903-22-4 (pbk.)
        I. Title. II. Series: LeDrew, Matthew, 1984- . Black womb.
PS8623.E424G56 2014   C813'.6   C2014-903827-5

Distributed by:
Engen Books
www.engenbooks.com
submissions@engenbooks.com

First mass market paperback printing: October 2010
Second mass market paperback printing: January 2015
Third mass market paperback printing: June 2019

Cover Image: Kit Sora Photography

For Ellen

PROLOGUE

Wednesday, Day Twenty-Two

You never know when your life is going to change, Xander thought as a glob of blood traveled down his throat.

He had to swallow at least once every few seconds, or the red fluid spraying from the artery in the roof of his mouth would start to flow out past his lips. His eyes were foggy, and he tried desperately to hold his guts inside of him, his throbbing intestines threatening to spill out onto the floor.

Blackness was melting off of him and dripping onto the dull concrete floor. Blood flowed by his feet, rushing to a drain in the center of the room.

His head weaved back and forth from exhaustion and dizziness, but he managed to hazard a glance toward the officers that lay around him. Some were missing limbs. The rest were missing heads. He felt their blood wash past his feet, and as he did, his eyes went to another victim.

Adam Genblade lay on the floor. A long, slender pipe had been shoved into his gut, and his face was covered with so many bruises and cuts that it was nearly unrecognizable. His orange jumpsuit was tainted red and stuck tightly to his skin, making it easy to see that he was not breathing. *You never know when fate is going to jump up and bite you in the ass and say: "I can't believe you didn't see that one coming." Because that's the worst part of sitting here... I really should have seen it coming.*

As his vision began to fail and he could feel himself slipping away, he looked up at the hulking figure that had done all of this, and his eyes filled with fresh terror at the renewed sight of the squirming form of black flesh and teeth and claws. Its mouth alone was bigger than Xander's entire body.

Uttering one last attempt at breath, Xander fell, his body crashing to the floor and his eyes rolling back into his head. His last thought was wondering how he'd let this sneak up on him. How he'd let his entire world come crashing down around his ears, when he'd had so long to stop it...

CHAPTER ONE:
THERAPY

TWENTY-ONE DAYS EARLIER

Wednesday, Day One

Three thick file folders slapped down onto Robert Snyder's desk. He jumped with fright and his hand jolted against the paperwork he'd been absorbed in, making the pen bump and scratch his name. He stared at the files for a moment, his eyes scanning over their pastel yellow covers, as if he was unsure of where they had come from as he woke up from his trace-like state. He turned his head to look to the person who had thrown them there, the lights above him reflecting off of his bald, egg-shaped crown and illuminating the backs of his ears, making him appear cartoonish. "Is there something I can help you with?" he asked calmly, but his voice was small and curt. He spoke down to people out of nature now, barely even realizing that he was doing it.

Warren O'Toole looked down at him, his arms crossed and his mouth taut with determination. His typically pleasant smile and demeanor were gone now, replaced by a grim, single-minded man's scowl. His black hair was matted and misplaced. The light coming in from a big bay window reflected off his glasses, which might as well have been telescopes that made his eyes impossible to see.

"Have a look," O'Toole said finally, gesturing one hand toward the files before taking his arms out of their crossed position and leaning both palms against the desk. He stared Snyder down. "Go ahead. Have a look and try to tell me that I didn't tell you so."

Snyder kept his cool, twining his fingers together as he straightened himself in his seat. A bone cracked somewhere in the center of his back, giving the troll-like man a momentary sense of relaxation. "Why don't you save me the trouble and tell me what's in them?" he responded coyly, sticking out his tongue a little as he spoke like a cobra hissing at a small mouse. "Something tells me I'm going to hear it anyway."

O'Toole's nostrils flared and he fought to keep his face from turning red with anger. He looked down at the files and flipped the top one open. A harsh black and white picture jumped out at the principal, making him balk.

It was a picture of Frederick Windser, taken shortly after he'd been shot a few days ago in the halls of the school by another student, Randy Owchar. Both of them once belonged to rival gangs, the Tees and the Omegas, respectively. Randy was still loose on the streets, and Frederick was buried in the ground, far too deep, it seemed, for anyone to remember.

"This is a police file on the murder of Windser," O'Toole stated, flipping through the pages methodically, slowly exposing close-up shots of different areas of the young man's body to Snyder's increasingly disgusted face, like a sick slide show.

"I can see that!" the principal snapped, rising slightly in his chair as the skin on the back of his hands became rough with goosebumps.

"Good for you," O'Toole quipped, shooting him a look. "Beneath it are two of my own folders on both Windser and Owchar, along with the information on them compiled by Phillips, the previous counselor," he informed Snyder as he continued flipping through the grotesque photos of the dead teenager. He'd made it as far as the morgue photos now. The boy had been sliced open from chest to pubic bone and spread wide with clamps to get at the bullet that had killed him, lodged just to the right of his spine.

Snyder's hand snapped forward with one quick motion, slapping the folder shut. "Is there a point to all this?" he yelled, saliva squirting from the gap between his two front teeth and making small, round water spots on the papers he'd been signing.

"I believe the point is that a young boy is dead, Principal Snyder," O'Toole responded coldly.

"I know that!" the smaller man protested, throwing his hands up a little, his face becoming one of pleading. "Don't you think I know that? All I've been doing for the last four days is sign papers and sheets and legal documents and ward off lawsuits and try to explain to lawyers that our board does not *believe* in metal detectors and..." he huffed, burying his nearly hairless head in his hands. "I know all that, Warren," he sighed, his voice sounded defeated. "Just tell me why you're in my office, reminding me of it all, when I've just spent the last four days trying to forget."

O'Toole frowned, his features softening for the first time since entering the office as he watched the man plead. He relaxed himself, then sat in the chair across from the principal. When he spoke, he hesitated to first make sure that his voice was even and fair, and in no way as accusatory as it had been at first. "I'm here because it could have been prevented," he explained, his voice a near whisper as he reached out and opened the file on Randy Owchar, pointing to a long list of dates and times. "I've called that boy into my office once every day since I got here, sir. Look," he motioned, pointing to another column, this time actually gaining Snyder's attention. "His grades had been slipping, his attendance record was almost nonexistent... This kid was textbook. He was another Derek Smith, and we all should have seen it. I asked you *thirteen times* to force him into regular therapy appointments. And before me, Phillips asked you ten times."

"I told you. It violates board policy. Besides, what if we hadn't gotten parental consent? You've never met that boy's parents, Warren. I have. Believe me, the last thing they'd want is a teacher telling them what went on inside their son's head."

"But we could have stopped it," O'Toole sighed, reaching down and holding up a large stack of files that he'd concealed beneath his chair when he came in.

"What's that?"

"This?" O'Toole responded in mock surprise, pointing at the stack of no less than twenty folders. "These are the folders of each of the other students who have either been refusing therapy, or have been attending but show signs of snapping."

Snyder turned white.

"Three more have been added to this pile since Fred Windser was killed, and I expect a few more by the end of the week," he said, flipping through the folders.

Snyder sighed heavily, his eyes darting back down to the paper he'd been signing to deny the school's responsibility. Now he wasn't so sure if he wanted his name on it. "What must be done?"

Warren smiled a little, his eyes shrinking a little as his cheeks pushed up. "I need to be able to force the students with probable cause to commit violent acts into counseling."

"Force?" Snyder repeated, his voice speaking volumes of his distaste for the word and its placement here.

Warren raised his hands in defense. "What I mean is, order them to come to me on a regular basis under penalty of suspension or expulsion, regardless of parental consent."

"That'd be difficult."

"So is cleaning blood stains off the hall tile."

Snyder closed his eyes and took a few long, deep breaths. He sighed. "Do whatever you have to," he said calmly, shaking his head in disbelief of his own words. When he opened his eyes again, they stared menacingly at Warren. "But so help me, keep it within reason, or you'll be the one who needs help."

O'Toole ignored the comment, the smile on his face wide as he scooped up all of his files and turned to walk out the door. As soon as he was outside the office and in the vacant halls of the school, he flipped through his fold-

ers eagerly, finding a thick one and holding it up, beaming at it.

Across the top, in bright red letters, read: Drew, Alexander.

CHAPTER TWO:
LINES IN THE SAND

"Yes!" Xander announced, letting a laugh slip through his lips as he finished keying in the start-up codes for his computer. He spun around in his chair and clapped his hands high in the air as his computer started to boot-up without major errors for the first time in three months.

It had taken a new hard drive, a new fan, a new motherboard and the replacement of every circuit wire in the entire box, but it was finally finished. The browser appeared on his screen with the tiny blue and white animation on the bottom telling him that everything was going fine. When his desktop finally loaded, it showed the bare minimum. All of his files were gone, all of his hacking programs, all of his games. Even some higher-up functions weren't operating and would have to be loaded from the system CD, but he had a computer, he had Internet, and everything else was fine, as far as he was concerned.

Slipping into his old habits, he pushed back his shaggy, dark brown hair, and dragged the mouse pointer down to the bottom right corner and clicked on the (miraculously) still-operating messenger service. A blue screen popped up with a small blinking red circle in one corner to tell him that he was online. Instinctively, he opened up his contacts list. His screen name started to bounce back and forth along the top of the screen, and the others slowly came into view as the computer checked them.

One stood out among the rest.

The screen name was 'baby_gurl'; it had been Sara Johnson's online tag from the time she was twelve years old until the day of her death. He stared at it long and hard, focusing on it until it seemed to pop out of the screen at him.

He turned to the left, gazing out of his bedroom window.

Her house was there; her bedroom window almost directly across from his. The lights were off, but if he tried hard enough he could imagine the soft glow of her monitor, which meant she would be online. Maybe she'd even notice him and give him a little wave. Then she'd sit down at her computer and pop a fresh piece of gum into her mouth. A few seconds later, he would hear a chime coming from his computer as she sent him a message, probably making fun of him for something he'd done in school that day. Or who she had a crush on now, and how it wasn't him. Or how crappy everything in their lives was. Or how she couldn't wait till tomorrow, so she could live another day of her crappy, little life.

He closed his eyes, forcing his gaze away from the window and back to the screen. When he opened his eyes again, her screen name was beckoning to him. He half expected to hear a rhythmic chime as she messaged him.

But, of course, she didn't.

Huffing, he brought the pointer up to her name and double-clicked it. A 'send message to' window came into view, overlapping the one that was already there. Frowning at himself, he felt the palms of his hands rest comfortably against the edges of his desk, his long fingers outstretched over the keyboard, like settling into an old chair after a long time to find that it was still grooved to fit your form. He took one deep breath, then started to type:

HEY SARA, I HAVEN'T SEEN YOU
IN A WHILE. JUST WANTED TO
WRITE AND ASK IF EVERYTHING WAS-

He stopped, then backspaced the entire passage, grunting to himself before starting again:

DEAR SARA, ITS BEEN TOO LONG
SINCE I'VE SEEN YOUR FACE. I MISS
YOU SO MUCH THAT IT KILLS ME
EVERY DAY, THINKING ABOUT
WHAT I ALMOST HAD, AND NOW
HAVE TO LIVE WITHOUT. JULIE
HAS BEEN-

He stopped, pushing the keyboard away in frustration, this time closing the dialog box. "Idiot," he chided.

-RING!-

He started in his chair as the phone rang downstairs. He then took a deep breath and composed himself after a moment, laughing. He brought the white mouse arrow up to Sara's screen name and right clicked it, moving down a long list of options until he reached *delete contact*. Hesitating just for a second, he pressed it, and she disappeared from the screen.

He stared at it for a moment, as if not understanding what he'd done.

His eyes darted over the screen, fluttering about and waiting for it to somehow magically reappear, but it did not.

His head dropped and he turned off the screen, then stood up and moved to the bed.

"Xander?" his mother called up from downstairs.

He sighed, rolling his eyes. "Yeah, Mom?"

"That was someone from your school on the phone. They said that you have to go into the school therapist's office instead of Technology tomorrow morning."

Xander sat up at the side of his bed, staring off into the darkness for a minute, feeling it around him. "Great," he said, then laughed a little. "Why would I need a therapist?"

⋏⋏

Mike Harris lay with his head on the soft pillow of his bed, his short blonde hair messy from a long night's sleep. Despite the early hour, he felt his eyes shutting as if they were weighed down by anchors, resistant to his efforts to keep them open. The soft light of early evening beamed in through the creases in his window blinds, providing just enough light for him to see the small girl using his chest for a pillow, the beating of his heart having lulled her to sleep.

Her name was Cathy Kennessy, and he had no doubt that she was the love of his life. As her dark, almost black hair tickled his nose and dared him to sneeze, she sighed gracefully in her sleep, a magical smile spreading across her lips. Her cheek was squished into his body, and she looked irresistibly cute. The top of her head was incredibly kissable, so he kissed it. In that moment she stirred, and he cursed himself a thousand times in his mind. Her dark eyes fluttered open in the pale blue light that softened her face and body, and she looked up at him, her eyes filled with beauty and peace.

"Hi," she said. The sound almost did not emerge, and when it did, it was small and fragile, like a mouse.

He smiled back at her, the arm that had been holding her tight to his body as she slept, squeezing her just a little tighter now in a lover's grasp. As if trying to hold onto love, to create a tangible something from that which is forever intangible. "Hi," he responded, beaming.

"Ugh," she groaned, laughing a little as her free hand reached up to pat down frizzy hair -- her vanity showing for only a moment. "How bad is it? Do I have crow's nest hair?"

He chuckled, making her still tired head bounce upon his chest as it heaved. "No," he assured her warmly, although her head looked like a mullet from those cheesy 80s hair bands where the singers didn't so much sing as scream. "You look amazing."

She rolled her eyes. "Yeah, I'm so..." she stopped, rethinking her sarcastic response in the spirit of the moment. "Okay, sure," she smiled to one side of her mouth, shrugging and re-nuzzling her head against his shoulder. "Amazing it is."

He stroked his hand through her long, flowing hair and watched as trace amounts of light got caught in it, trapped by this young woman's sweetness. The world stood still, and the only sound in the universe was their slow breathing in unison.

There was a long pause between them that said everything in the world. It spoke of the bond between them that could been seen for miles by blind men. Of the pain that they crawled through and still came out pure and whole on the other side. Of the love that bonded them and would continue to bond them no matter how many miles apart they were from each other. In their minds and their hearts, they would always be one, lying alone in the twilight, hearing nothing but one another's heartbeat.

"You know what tomorrow is, right?" he asked glumly, the words escaping him in the form of a deep-throated sigh.

"Yeah," she said, playing with his chest with one finger, dragging it along and scraping at the skin lightly with her nail. "I know."

"Are you okay?"

She smiled, moving her head to look up at him. "Yes," she said definitively, as though commanding it to be true. "Yeah, I'll be fine."

"How do you think he'll be?"

She paused, frowning. "I'm not quite sure. You never can be with him. I think it's safe to say it won't be good. He still hasn't gotten over it."

Mike shook his head, correcting her. "Yes, he has," he argued, stroking the side of her face until she quickly kissed him playfully. "As much as a man can, anyway."

"Now," Warren O'Toole said in an authoritative voice,

"pay attention to what I'm telling you to do."

All traces of the man's kindness were gone. The walls that he'd built to deal with stupid, immature children had vanished, and he was now more like a drill sergeant. He no longer had to coax the young man in front of him to do anything. He had the authority, and he chose to use it.

Xander lay on the long, oblong couch that had been clumsily shoved up against the far wall of O'Toole's office, his hands folded at his chest, mocking the position he'd seen in so many movies. "Oh, come on now," he smirked. "Is that how Robin Williams got Will to open up?"

"This isn't *Good Will Hunting*, Mr. Drew," O'Toole reminded him curtly, as he fiddled loudly with things outside of Xander's view. "And even if that were the case, you are neither a closet genius nor a beaten adolescent," he drawled, walking over to Xander and sitting on the cheap chair next to the couch. It was flimsy and threatened to give out under the thin man's weight. He looked at Xander for a long moment, appearing tired and worn out. He looked like a man who hadn't slept in weeks.

Xander sighed. "So, how do we do this?" he said, trying desperately not to make it sound like a groan.

O'Toole smiled at Xander's compliance, although it had to be forced out of him. He reached into the breast pocket of his faded blue shirt, pulling out a gold pocket watch. "I'll be placing you into a hypnotic state, Mr. Drew. While in that - "

"With that?" Xander said, raising an eyebrow and pointing at the pocket watch. It spun on the end of its chain, but an engraving could still be made out: *To Warren, for many years of loyal service.*

"Excuse me?" O'Toole stuttered, trying to find his words after being interrupted.

"You're seriously going to try and hypnotize me... with a pocket watch?" Xander laughed skeptically.

Warren smiled, dangling the golden chain confidently. "Why, yes, actually."

Xander laughed, covering his mouth with one hand. "Okay, enough. That's funny. What, am I on Candid Camera or something?"

O'Toole frowned, rubbing his free hand through his hair and grabbing it. "No, Mr. Drew. You're not on Candid Camera. Although I'm starting to think that this seems more and more like that kind of situation, don't you?"

Xander squinted his eyes at the older man. "You're really serious, aren't you?"

"That's what I've been telling you."

The younger man clicked his tongue against the roof of his mouth a couple of times, letting saliva slosh in and out of the gap between his two front teeth. "Can I see it first?"

O'Toole smiled wide, handing him the trinket.

Xander held it in the palm of his hand, watching as the light from the desk lamp gleamed off of its gold-plated surface. He bit his lip as he saw his own reflection in it, and could almost picture himself transforming. He could almost feel the beast inside of him breaking down barriers, clawing at the doors of his consciousness, waiting, wanting. Wanting the blood. As Xander stared at the watch, he thought he could hear O'Toole's heartbeat get louder and louder until it was all he could hear; like a soft drink machine with 'drink me' scrawled across it.

"I'd like to have that back now," O'Toole coughed, reaching out and grabbing the watch by its chain. "Is there anything else before we begin?"

Xander stared forward, his eyes still glued to the gold that was swinging before his eyes. He nodded despite himself, sweat starting to bead on the top of his forehead. "What kinds of things are you going to ask me?" he said suddenly, as the doctor leaned into place.

O'Toole ignored the young man, and began dangling the watch in front of his face. Already, Xander's eyes were getting heavy, his pulse slowing. "Watch only the watch," O'Toole instructed him, his voice forcibly monotone and flat. "Listen only to my voice."

Xander closed his eyes reluctantly. After a moment, his breathing became steady as he drifted into a deep, heavy sleep...

ʎʎ

Julie Peterson watched with vibrant green eyes as the clock on the classroom wall slowly ticked away, each second feeling like an hour. She tried to distract herself from the long winded teacher as she went on to no end about logarithmic functions and how they might actually have some use in the real world, and they weren't just invented to make students fail eighth grade math. Julie filtered everything out until the chatter of students, the droning of the teacher, and the shuffling of desks and chairs all melded together to form a hum that she was apart from; beyond, even. And in the instant that she transcended the classroom, all she could think about was him.

Dr. Darren Phillips.

Posing as a guidance counselor, Phillips used his position to figure out which young girls were emotionally unstable and prey upon them with two of his friends.

They chose her first.

While on her way home from school one day, they slowed down next to her in their car, jumped out and shoved her into the alleyway that her bedroom window looked out on. They punched her, kicked her, tore off her clothes and left them around her, like shreds of her sanity blowing around in the wind. Each of them took a turn and climbed on, one by one. They killed a part of her, emotionally and physically. Physically, they demolished the part of her that would allow her to carry on. The part of her that could better herself, and give a new and beautiful life to the world. With their feral, carnal rage plunging in and out of her, they destroyed any hope for her future of having children.

One boy helped put Phillips away where the sun would never be able to touch his face again. To a place so far away that she could feel safe and secure and not be afraid to look out her bedroom window and wonder if he was still there, watching and waiting: Xander Drew.

Now, she knew he was in the hands of the latest guidance counselor. He was under the older man's influence, and she couldn't help but to be terrified by that thought. The thought that something so terrible might happen to him, like it did to her. Because, despite what everyone said, and despite what her own head was telling her, she found herself falling in love with Alexander Drew a little more every day.

She took a deep breath and looked down at the notepad in front of her, only now realizing that she had been subconsciously etching Xander's name into the brittle lined paper. She turned the page quickly, but it was still there. She'd pressed so hard that the imprint of his name was left on the next sheet, just like he'd been imprinted upon all of her thoughts.

I hate this place. She thought suddenly, looking around at the student body that surrounded her. *I hate what it's done to Xander, to me... to Mandy.*

Mandy Peterson; Julie's thirteen-year-old cousin. On her first day living with Julie and her mother, Mandy had been captured in the night by a group of fanatics calling themselves the Tees. Something had saved her... she wouldn't say what - just made up a wild story about a 'black angel' that had taken hold of her and made everything all right. *There isn't a person in this town that hasn't been hurt or scared in some way... but they all pretend like it doesn't happen. And by doing so, they make you pretend. They give you this look when you try to speak out, like you're insane. They don't want you to shatter their fantasy about what their town is like. And I hate them for it. And I wonder...* she thought, rubbing a hand through her shoulder length brown hair in frustration as she began to scratch his name in blue onto her pad again. *What terrible thing is it that Alexander Drew is hiding from everyone, and when will it come out?*

It sat in the woods just north of the more populated areas of town, fidgeting and twitching a little. It was covered in blood and saliva, the latter its own, the former not. Its great lungs heaved in and out as its body struggled for air, winded from the exertion and near sexual pleasure of the hunt. In one of its great hands it held what remained of a young golden lab, its tiny form still hot from the blood that streamed from the gaping gash in its shoulder and back. The creature raised its treat to its lips again. Massive jaws spread so wide that there was a snapping sound as they dislocated. It revealed three rows of long, razor sharp teeth that sparkled in the light that escaped between the oak branches enveloping the beast, concealing it from the world outside. It took the head and upper body of the infant dog this time, its strong mouth snapping the tiny bones of the pup's spine and rib cage, squirting more blood and spinal fluid into the killer's mouth. As it chewed briefly and then swallowed, its large, red eyes began to dissect the wilderness around it, instinctively searching out something new.

It was hungry.

Xander woke, his sinuses filled with a throbbing pain that seemed to grow bigger and more frustrating with every beat of his heart. Everything was dark, and he couldn't see one foot in front of his face, save for a thick mist that seemed to cover everything. It was like being inside steam, and to his horror, there didn't seem to be any discernible floor for him to stand upon either. It was like being gas, his body as weightless as a feather frolicking in the summer wind. He turned his head quickly, and when he did, his features seemed to distort and skew. Everything was blurry. When he moved his hands, it looked like he had eighteen fingers. He could feel the blood coursing through his body, and each beat of his heart brought pain.

"No..." he said softly, biting his lip as he craned his head, trying to find some small source of light to fixate on, to let his eyes gain focus. He turned, and came face to face with himself.

The other version of himself was dripping blood from his nose and mouth, and stared blankly at his reflection. The beaten, bloodied version of him seemed to fade backward until Xander could see the full scene of what was happening. Then he knew exactly where he was. He was staring at himself upon a crucifix.

Blood was flowing from the sacrificed one's veins onto a barely lit panel of metal floor, and the entire scene seemed to hang there in the darkness. His eyes were rolling up into the back of his head, and the parts that were white had thick, prudent red vines developing at the base. His hands and feet were twitching violently under the enormous pressure of the three metal spikes that had been shoved through his legs and both wrists. It was a constant battle for the crucified young man to keep his head up, one that he was losing. His entire torso was covered in scars and bruises, and each one was like a memory: a painful, repressed memory that one only visited when forced to.

He picked Xander up, propping him up against the wall. He took out a small, sharp blade and jammed it into Black Womb's right side. A soft -shink- sound indicated that it went clean through the wall. Genblade let go of Womb, letting the blade prop him. "There's a few things you should know, Womb. Number one..."

Shunk. *Genblade stabbed Xander in the arm.*

Xander winced in real time, the recollection of that feeling coming back to him. But more than that, he fell over. When he looked at his arm, blood was erupting from his arteries like a fountain.

"... your right side is your weak spot. It's where your true self... the real Black Womb... resides. But you probably figured that out. Number two..."

Shunk. *He stabbed him through his other arm.*

Xander opened his mouth to scream, but no words would come out. He gripped the new wounds at once, his mind torn as to which gaping hole to clutch, which arm felt like it needed to be torn off more.

"... that healing factor of yours will only go so far. If you tax it too much... or if I do... it'll simply cut out. Number three..."

Shunk. *He stabbed him through both feet, pinning them to each other and to the wall.*

Xander fell now, into the blackness. For a moment, he thought that he might plunge into the shadows forever, an eternity of awaiting death at the end of some bottomless pit. Then his head slammed into concrete, followed by the rest of his body. He impacted the ground like a bag of stones, and his entire body ached for a long time; he wasn't sure how long.

"... nobody. I repeat, NOBODY, escapes death."

Genblade stepped back and admired his work. Black Womb hung there, his body pinned into a cross position. Black Womb's mind reeled. He couldn't focus on anything, his vision was blurry, and black around the edges. He felt the healing factor cut out. He lifted his head to face his attacker.

"A crucifixion," Genblade sneered. "It'd almost be poetic, if it wasn't so damn funny."

When Xander decided to move, he pushed off of the floor with all the force he could muster, which was just enough to roll himself over. His chest rose and fell violently as his lungs struggled for oxygen. Blood bubbled to the surface of the blunt force stab wounds that were scattered over his body -- each stab surrounded by a ring of contusions. As he lay on his back, struggling for air, the lights came on. He didn't need them to, they just did. He didn't need to see the dome-shaped metallic ceiling, or the flat, square fluorescent lights, or the observation window that the people in charge used to look down upon experiments. He didn't even need to see the creases of the nearly hidden doorway that would soon be his exit. As soon as he'd seen himself on the cross, he knew there was only one place on earth that he could be.

Engen.

"No..." he said again, and in his mind, both words were spoken simultaneously. But as the growing puddle of blood around him would testify, he'd been there for at least an hour, perhaps more. He shook his head in rebellion, pouting his lower lip. He closed his eyes tightly and wished for it not to be true, but when

he opened them, he was still there. "No, not here again!" he screamed, begging the walls that did nothing except echo back at him. He groaned. "Not death again. I've been here once before... and escaped. I don't want to be here. I shouldn't be here. I have... places to be..."

The watch dangled in front of his face, reflecting light and blinding him.

He blinked hard, and it was gone. It was just him, all alone, again. Clutching his head tightly to keep it from throbbing, he slowly sat up and rubbed the back of his head. He turned to look at himself, or rather what appeared to be a representation of himself, hanging a few feet from the floor, all of the blood draining from his body. He reached out and touched the steady stream of the blood of his past that ran toward the drain in the center of the sloped floor.

His hand passed through it, but more importantly, it passed through his hand.

The red liquid did not change its course to avoid his flesh, it simply passed right through it. "I don't know how I got here this time," Xander spoke, running the scenario through his head over and over again, trying to recall how he had gotten there. He rubbed his thumb and forefinger together, verifying that there was no trace of blood there. He looked over at his cru-cified self, frowning with pity as though he were looking upon an old friend that he no longer remembered. "But, I sure as hell know how he got here."

He reached out and almost touched the bleeding, sagging form of himself, who didn't even seem to recognize his presence there. The body twitched as it neared unconsciousness, mak-ing Xander's arm recoil in fear as he regarded the bleeding man with a strange pathos.

"It was months ago now. Maybe longer, maybe shorter. Who knows, really. When the story of your life reads like mine, dates and times tend to fade into the background so far that they become void. Everything was going great... even though I didn't realize it at the time. Back then, I thought my life was crap. Less than crap. My life gave crap a bad name. Got beat up all the time at school, Sara was my best friend and that was never going to change, and even Mike and Cathy wouldn't publicly admit to having been my friends. Yeah, everything was terrible... but I'd have given anything to have it all back again. Because then the day came that everything changed. The day that Jamie Dawkins died.

"Then again, 'died' is a pretty loose term for what happened to Jamie. He was found eviscerated in an alley just after he and Sara were supposed to hook up. Every major organ aside from his tar-ridden lungs had been snatched. After that, everything started to read like a horror novel.

"Looking back, it seems like everything was counting down to that one moment when everything exploded. Like my life was a ticking time bomb, and the shockwave took out everyone and everything closest to me. The big boom: Julian Grendel's party-of-the-century. So, as the bodies kept piling up and Mike and Cathy were added to the critical list, everyone else pretended that the world was normal... even me. At Grendel's party, the moment I'd been waiting almost fifteen years for happened: Sara kissed me. Well, almost. I got called off to help with a computer problem, being the resident nerd and all. Sara waited outside for me... but somebody else had been waiting too.

"Ten minutes later, Grendel tried to rape Cathy, Mike had been beaten into unconsciousness, and I was at the bottom of the stairs, victim to a mob who thought I was the person killing all of their friends. And Sara... Sara was hanging from a ceiling fan, her entrails falling out of her violated body onto the blood-spattered hardwood floor.

"When I woke up, I was here. At Engen. This is where I met the man who changed my life: Adam Genblade. He told me the truth, or at least his edited version of it. I'd been the one killing the students in my school; I attacked Mike and Cathy -- everything. It had been me. All because when I was still inside my mother's womb, Engen geneticists had implanted me with a darkness. A blackness that had the potential for the worst power known to man. They'd given me the Black Womb.

"But there was something wrong. My personality had fractured and splintered, leaving me as two people living in one body. When I slept, Black Womb woke. It ripped itself out of my veins, pouring black ooze all over my body until it covered me with a scaly second skin. This thing was acting on my deepest desires, like an impressionable child wanting to impress mommy and daddy.

"Engen wanted me back. They wanted their living weapon. But they didn't want me. They knew that I would never work for them, not after they helped me put Sara in the ground. They wanted the organ. He wanted it. Alpha, one of the worst minds ever to have existed. He needed the Womb's healing factor to make himself whole again. To use my incredible power to rain down fire upon the world."

Xander looked at his reflection, and his heart sank.

"Given the chance, I'd take my old life back in a minute, compared to this."

Suddenly, his reflection looked up, making eye contact with him. It spat out a bit of blood before sneering at Xander. "Oh, shut the fuck up," it drawled, pulling its arms and legs free of the spikes that pinned it to the wall, landing gracefully upon the cold metal floor. It rose up, staring Xander right in the eye. *"Do you always whine this much? I don't remember ever hearing somebody yammer on so self-indulgently before."*

Xander stepped back, shocked. He raised his hand to strike, but then let it hang in midair, awaiting answers. "What the hell are you?"

"Don't you recognize me?" the other Xander smiled evilly, using one nail to scrape a bit of dried blood from his lips. *"Here,"* he smirked, stepping forward and grabbing Xander's hand, *"maybe this'll help."* He pulled Xander's clenched fist to his gut, and Xander was horrified to watch the tip of a sword punch out the other side, spraying blood and shards of human flesh against the wall. When he looked down, he saw that the hand his ghost had forced was now holding the grip of a sword. The spider-sword, to be exact, encrusted with gold and rubies to shape a deadly blood-red spider.

"This didn't happen," Xander whispered, confused.

The second Xander pushed the first, sending him flying to the floor, bumping his tail bone violently. *"You're a Womb, kid. You gotta stop living in the past. This is the now,"* he said, but his voice had adopted a soothing, feminine quality to it. It was like spring time. The Ghost-Xander took the sword out of himself, twirling it around majestically as black ooze erupted from the gaping hole going right through him, transforming him. But as he transformed, his flesh re-imagined itself, not into the red-eyed, over-bitten Black Womb, but into a small, muscular feminine body. Almond eyes formed, and a sly pair of black lips that were locked in a sinister smile appeared. She was scantily clothed in red silk; a gust of wind in either direction would have exposed her voluptuous form.

"Spider lives," she said sarcastically, turning and pointing the sword at Xander's throat. "Your life is so horrible... well, at least you're alive. The part of the story that you seem to like leaving out was when you killed me, stuck me through and through with my own blade."

"It was in self-defense," Xander protested.

"Semantics. I was just following orders."

"You enjoyed it."

Spider paused, her smile spreading further. "Yeah, I did," she chuckled. "But you have no reason to bitch anymore. You know it wasn't you that killed all of your friends now... just one or two of them." Her skin morphed, and she became a male again, with scruffy brown hair. Her voice stayed the same, but she was still Derek Smith. "It wasn't Genblade either. It was your own friend who killed all your little buddies: Derek. So, why are you still blaming us? Why are you still saying that we're responsible for everything?"

"Because you are. You started this, you woke it up," Xander snarled, his shock having transformed into anger as Spider transformed into Smith.

"We didn't start it, sweetie," Spider grinned, resuming her own form. "And if it wasn't for us, I guess you wouldn't have had the opportunity to stop all the evil around you, anyway. You shouldn't be cursing us... you should be thanking us."

"I'm not cursing you -- you cursed me."

"Yeah," she snarled sarcastically before changing again, this time into a young female: Julie Peterson, tiny freckles and all. "And I suppose you would've been able to save your little girl-friend from the perverted guidance counselor if Engen hadn't given you your power, hmm? And Derek, and Blackheart, and Roulette... you think we've caused death by creating you? Your 'evil' Womb has done more good in a few short months than you did in fifteen years hunched over your computer. So, why don't you think before you start throwing around..."

"Get out!" Xander barked at Spider, getting up off of the floor and brushing himself off.

"Excuse me?" Spider-as-Julie said, raising an eyebrow. "You're the one who came here, remember? Don't tell me to leave."

The watch dangled in front of his face, reflecting light and blinding him.

"Get out of that body," Xander exclaimed, taking one menacing step toward Spider.

Spider hummed happily, amused at the torment she was instilling. She began rubbing her hands all over Julie's body, changing the clothes as she went until she was wearing the little red night gown that Julie had once used in an attempt to seduce Xander prematurely. "What's the matter, Alex?" she said, her voice sounding like Julie's now. "Don't you want me? Aren't I good enough for you? Why can't you love me?" She broke out into an infectious giggle, Spider's giggle. "And you said your life had petty problems before. All you've done for weeks now is swoon over the first sweet young thing to jump you in a hotel room. Yeah, you've matured so much. You're practically an adult."

"Get out of that body," Xander repeated, ordering her in a tone of voice so forceful it surprised even him.

Spider smiled at him with Julie's lips. "Have it your way," she said, transforming again. "Maybe I was wrong. Maybe there's a different stupid teenager you've got the hots for."

She grew short blonde hair, and the freckles and scars disappeared to reveal perfect, flawless skin and a ruby smile.

It was Sara.

Xander began to tremble, his form losing its edges. His lower lip began to quiver, and he fell to his knees on the ground before his love, the tears beginning to roll down his face.

"There, there, lover," Sara soothed in her musical voice, crouching next to him and pulling his head into her breast, stroking the hair on the back of his head. "Calm down. I'm right here, Xander. You must have had a terrible dream, sweetheart. It's okay now."

She closed her eyes, kissed him once on the forehead, then laid him back onto the cold floor and started to sing him to sleep.

"Tora Lora Lora, tora Lora lye.

Tora Lora Lora, hush now don't you cry.

Tora Lora Lora, tora Lora lye.

That's an Irish lullaby."

He smiled, then turned to face her, his eyes sparkling the way they hadn't in months. When he looked, he was lying next to Spider.

She stabbed him with her sword once in the gut, then shoved him away with more force than the assassin had ever wielded in life, sending him skidding across the floor. "Is that how you think it is?" she laughed, standing above Xander and pushing the tip of her blade toward him until his chest bled from its wound. "She won't choose you, you know," she grinned, kneeling down to get closer to him. "None of them will, in the end. Because the only person you've ever picked for your lover is death. The only people that will ever take you in are the angels, boy. The angels in the darkness with their wings of blood and feathers of fire, mount their horses, the four of them will... the other two can fly, you see."

"What are you rambling about, now?" Xander spat, masking his obvious pain with annoyance.

She raised a hand to her face, and was about to speak, when Xander cut her off.

"Let me guess," he said, raising his hand to interject. "Scar tissue, right?"

"It'll heal, lover."

"Do you have to insist on calling me that?"

"But sweetheart..." she laughed, leaning in and giving him a kiss. "I was your first."

Xander looked confused, bewildered. "Um, but we've never..."

She drew back and slapped him with an open palm across the face. "Not sex, stupid. Kill. I was your first kill. The first that you did all on your own, without any help from your precious little Black Womb. You did me all on your own... the first of many."

"I've never killed anyone since you. The Womb's committed all the murders I've done since Engen."

"But you will, my love," she cooed softly, straddling his waist. "You'll kill more than Alpha, Genblade, and me combined. Because you have something we don't. Something you share with Derek and all the others."

"What's that?"

"You, my boy, have the capability for real evil. Even before you were a Womb, you sat at home at night and fantasized about killing every red blooded male on the earth so that your magnificent Sara might actually have you... although, it's more likely she would have gone gay rather than date you. Engen may have created the Womb, boy... but you gave birth to it."

"Argh!" Xander yelled, flipping Spider off of him and jumping up into a fighting stance, ready for an attack.

She merely sat on the floor and laughed, her legs spread toward him. "And just as I was your first, you'll be his first. His One. The first angel in the dark..."

"Shut up!" he yelled, clutching the sides of his head as if it were going to explode. "'Pain is my power,' 'angels in the dark,' will you stop talking in riddles. Just tell me what you're going to tell me and be done with it! I'm sick of all the mind games with you and your twisted little boyfriend Genblade!"

Spider looked solemn, then. Her eyes cast downward. "Adam," she whispered, her gaze becoming watery. "I fear that he will join me all too soon. Before his time."

Xander squinted, relaxing his stance to look at Spider, until his eyes grew wide with understanding. "Genblade?" he demanded, "Are you saying that something's going to happen to Genblade? Is he what's coming?"

Spider turned her head into the darkness that surrounded the both of them, and an image formed there. It was Adam Genblade, his eyes locked open as blood poured from every crevice in his body, and a few newly ripped ones. His face was covered in so many contusions that he was only identifiable by the orange prison jumpsuit that he wore. There was a pipe sticking out of his side, and blood was running out of it as if on tap. Judging by the amount of blood surrounding him, he was past the point of saving.

"No..." Xander gasped, walking toward the image until he touched it, and it vanished like fog. He closed his eyes tightly, clenching his fists. He frowned in determination. "So, Adam's gonna die, huh?" he said, hiding his own pain. "Wow, I'm hurting. Really, that's painful. I think I might have a moment."

Spider smiled through her tears, wiping them away. "You cannot hide yourself from me, Womb. We're siblings, you and I.

But even if you could let Adam fade to black... it would do you no good in the battle to come."

Xander squinted. "What battle?"

"Your greatest battle yet, and possibly ever. The battle that has been coming ever since you were given life and ripped from your mother's teat. You're going to lose everything, Womb: no family, no friends... not even Genblade to save you. And when it comes, you'll have nobody to blame but yourself. Somebody has let it out. And it's going to kill the world, Xander. It's going to make it bleed."

"Who?" Xander demanded, punching the air for effect. "What? Tell me what's coming!"

Spider looked sad, giving the Womb absolute grief. "You are."

ᚼᚼ

Xander's eyes snapped open as the small, golden pocket watch was taken away. O'Toole rubbed it with a small cloth for a moment, then tucked it back into his left breast pocket. He looked up to see that Xander was still laying there, blinking over and over again, as if to try and awaken himself.

"That was an excellent session," O'Toole beamed, almost patronizingly. He took off his glasses, revealing tiny, beady eyes, and used his handkerchief to wipe the lenses. "I think your unconscious mind reached many revelations about itself."

"Revelations?" Xander repeated, sitting up, his expression one of bewilderment as he rubbed an ache on the back of his neck.

"Yes, you seemed very calm. I used a few relaxation

techniques on you that should prove helpful toward alleviating the stress that most males your age enact upon their body and mind, even unconsciously," he explained, tucking away the rag and perching his glasses back upon his nose.

"Relaxation?"

"Mmm-hmm. I would have kept going, but I have another appointment that I'm eager to get underway. Can I expect to see you again soon?"

"You're forcing me into this."

"I know. I was just being polite. But, if you insist on being curt, I *will* see you again soon."

Xander frowned, getting up and stretching out a crick in his back until he heard it snap, then walked toward the door. When he opened it, Mandy Peterson was standing outside.

Her skin was flawless, devoid of any mark or blemish, except for one tiny m-shaped scar that was mostly hidden by her hairline. She could often be found in the girls' locker room applying makeup to the small bit of damaged tissue, complaining about its refusal to go away. The only thing really defining about the girl's face was its absence of color, making her look like she was wasting away. She had dark brown hair that came to her shoulders, and accented her deep green eyes. Her lips were small and delicate, and right now they were giving Xander her trademark infectious, toothy smile. She was wearing a tight tube top with a kitten in the center of the breasts and words that read: *Watch out, I bite*, along with bell-bottom jeans that were just a little too short for her, exhibiting a bit of leg.

"Hi, Alex!" she beamed, calling Xander by his given

name. It was a quirk that she'd picked up from her cousin, Julie, and now it seemed like a full time job just to explain to the both of them that he hated to be called that.

He forced a laugh, but it sounded mechanical. The gears in his head were beginning to turn about what Spider had been talking about in his vision. "Hey, Mandy," he smiled, "is your cousin around?"

"Julie? No, she was in class, then she stopped going to class and went for a smoke, then she came back from her smoke and went to another class, but I saw her in the hall and she said that she thought that the class was, like, boring, so she went out walking. First she went to the girl's room, but Snyder caught her in there, so then she left, and now I don't know where she is. Maybe she's in class. Or having a smoke. Or in the girl's room," Mandy took a breath after the long-winded speech, resuming her open-mouthed smile.

Xander stared at her, wide eyed, for a moment, then looked at the clock, and then at Warren O'Toole. "Right. One hour on the clock she's gonna be talking," Xander chuckled, almost feeling sorry for the counselor. "Have fun with your handful, buddy." He walked out, closing the door behind him.

"That reminds me!" Mandy's high-pitched voice said from behind the doorway. "I had another dream about that Black Angel guy last night, and it was so weird, but he kept speaking like someone I know..."

Xander stopped, stared at O'Toole's name on the door, then sighed and walked away.

CHAPTER THREE:
LOVER'S WALK

She danced in her backyard before dinner, her long, curly black hair waving about in the light of the low sun.

She wore a small, dark blue dress that seemed to catch even the most minute traces of wind, chilling her legs and making her shiver, even though she didn't really notice. Little Kerri Walker was no more than seven years old. She still didn't talk much, but the doctors had told her parents time and time again that there was nothing wrong with her. She'd just talk when she felt like talking, and that was all. When she did speak, her missing two front teeth caused her to have a lisp that all of the boys in her grade made fun of, even when the teachers yelled at them for it.

Her shoes were red and sparkly, something she had insisted upon after watching the *Wizard of Oz* for the thirtieth time. Every time she got mud on them, she'd scrape them through the wet grass repeatedly to clean them until the sparkles shone like diamonds, then tapped her heels together three times, repeating 'there's no place like home' with every tap. Her sea-green eyes regarded everything with interest, the freshness of seeing everything for the first time and finding wonder in it. Every time the trees outside of her house blew in the wind, she watched the leaves and branches in their fluid motion, brushing against each other and making a rustling sound like when her teacher crumpled up paper to throw in the garbage. Sometimes, leaves would escape from their branches in a strong breeze and float along on the wind a few minutes before touching the ground or getting stuck in the shrubs that her father tended to meticulously -- not out of enjoyment, but in competition with the neighbors and their gaudy lawn ornaments. She'd chase the leaves, jumping and clapping her hands together in an attempt to catch them, always missing, but never quitting. When they eventually met the ground tenderly, like daddy's lips on mommy's cheek, she'd pick them up and carefully place them in the sandbox, decorating it for just a little while until the wind grasped it again, or mom came out to clean up.

The wind whipped forward, blowing the trees again, this time swooping upward and revealing bits and pieces of the underbrush. For a moment, she thought she saw something red. Red and sparkling with life, just like her shoes. She smiled her little missing-tooth smile, walked over to the edge of the brush and peered in, pulling back branches to see what was sparkly. Her eyes were filled with that innocence and wonder of a child seeing something for the first time, never once dawning upon her that whatever it was might want to hurt her. Never thinking that anything bad could happen. She'd never been hurt before, and the very notion was so foreign to her it might as well have been in Oz.

She gazed around, but all she could see was blackness, even though the sun was still in the sky, illuminating the forest. Kerri jumped and grabbed a high evergreen branch, pulling it down. Two red, curved, triangular eyes peered out at her, having been watching her the entire time. She stared at it for a moment.

Its breathing was heavy, all of its long, sharp teeth tucked inside of its mouth. With one movement it grabbed her and pulled her into the cover of the brush outside of her home, time enough for only the tiniest yelp to escape from her mouth.

As it dragged her into the forest, it was all she could do to tap her shoes together between screams and whisper, "there's no place like home... there's no place like home... there's no place like home."

It was a simple slab of stone in a garden where mounds of carved rock seemed to sprout up like live trees that were fed by the dead and strangled sunlight from the living. The letters engraved upon it were still etched perfectly, as sharp and as definitive as they had been months ago when they were put there.

"I'm not really sure what to do here," Mike coughed, squeezing Cathy's hand as they both stared down at the grave of Sara Johnson. The debris of Fall passed by them on the same breeze that caught hold of Cathy's hair and did not seem to want to let go. "Is it always this noisy?"

"It's noisy?" Cathy said, her voice distant at first, then perking up with sarcasm as she raised an eyebrow in his direction. She turned away from the grave with a puzzled look on her face. "There isn't a sound here, Mike. It's a graveyard."

"Well, yeah," he admitted, shuffling around a little, looking at the ground on which he tread while making small circles with his feet in an odd, oval shaped pattern. "But, it's a talkative silence. It's like you can hear everything that all of these people *aren't* saying. All the things they could never say, but always wanted to. It's a noisy silence." He continued shuffling his feet until he realized he was messing up the soil atop his friend's grave, then quickly retracted his feet into a militaristic position.

Cathy stopped, her eyes slowly panning over the headstones that sprang up out of the ground like weeds in a garden. The names faded into the blackness just before dusk on even the brightest nights, casting sinister silhouettes and making the entire landscape look like nothing but crosses and angels. For a moment, she wondered if this was what heaven looked like, just as the sun set. "You're right," she agreed, nodding once before turning back to him. "It is noisy in here. You just have to figure out which voice is Sara's, then talk to her."

Mike made a guttural, scratchy sound deep in his throat. "That's the stupidest thing I've ever heard," he scoffed, pulling away from Cathy just a little. His eyes refused to even glance in the direction of his lost friend's grave. "She can't hear us, Cathy. She's dead! They killed her, then they buried her, and now she's a rotting corpse whose ears probably aren't even attached to her head!" he screamed, punching the air in front of him as he bellowed at the graves at the bottom of the hill.

Cathy just stood back and watched, both her index fingers pressed against her mouth, waiting for the time when he needed her to speak.

Chest heaving, he turned back to her, revealing a face full of molten-hot tears. He took a step forward, then collapsed onto Sara's grave. Open palms grabbed great handfuls of dirt, wishing that it were the smooth flesh of her shoulders as he held her in a tight embrace. The mud got under his nails and stained his hands as water from his body fed the earth, helping to give it the life he wished he could provide to his friend. "Why?' he said, softly at first, his voice cracking from tears. He pushed himself up on his knees, heaving the mounds of muck at the headstone, making huge splotches. "Why!" he screamed as loud as he could, eyes filled with hate. "I needed you, Sara! I needed you and you went away. You could have done anything else but that, and I would have stood by you, but do not expect me to forgive you for this!" he yelled, burying his face in his palms and covering it with dirt, not that he cared.

Cathy slowly walked up behind him, placing her hand on his shoulder at first, then wrapping her arms around his neck and squeezing him so hard that she thought her ribs might collapse, but she didn't care. "She loved you, you know," she assured him, kissing his neck lightly with every word she spoke.

Mike sniffed back the mucus in his nose, nodded, then wiped his eyes in her jacket. "I know," he said, pulling her even closer to him. Taking comfort in the smell of her skin, the way her long hair itched his nose when he got too close to it, and the way her slender neck looked up close, blurry and somehow sensual.

"*I* love you, too, you know," she said, her voice shaking like one of the leaves that blew around the churchyard, getting caught in the wire mesh fence that surrounded it.

It was kind of like her, thought Mike. *I built so many fences just to try and keep her out, to keep everybody out, so that I wouldn't have to deal with anything. So that I could keep myself separate from everything. But she manages to get herself into every part of my life, manages to touch it and make it better just for having been there, even if she never ventures back again. And if I put up a fence, she becomes a leaf and gets stuck in it, until that fence is just a wall made of her love... protecting me, instead of holding me in.* "I love you more," he said finally leaning in to give her a kiss.

"Believe me, that's not possible," she whispered, laughing a little.

"Oh, yes it is," he chuckled in return. "Just look up 'love' in the dictionary. You'll see a picture of us there, and I'll have a little plus sign above my head, indicating who loves who more."

"Funny," she smirked, giving him a look. "Do you have to be competitive about everything?"

He smiled warmly, gently brushing an eyelash away from her face. "Only you," he responded, turning to look at Sara's grave. "Yeah, Sar," he chuckled, "I know."

Cathy hugged him again. The chilled wind left them alone now. It knew it couldn't touch them anyway. "Come on," she coaxed, cocking her head toward the trail back to the road, "let's go for a walk. It's a nice night, shame to waste it."

The two of them got up and started walking back down the hill hand in hand, until Mike stopped. "Oh!" he exclaimed, giving himself a tap on the head. "Didn't you want to talk to Sara?"

Cathy smiled, shaking her head. "That's okay. She already knows what I was going to say."

〴〵

"Kerri!" called Macy Walker, her voice loud and shrill, probably waking all of the neighbors as she screamed out her back door from the small kitchen where she was mixing the batter for low fat muffins. More batter was on her than in the bowl, with splotches all over her face. She huffed and put down the mixing bowl, scrunching her forehead. "Kerri, it's time to get washed up and go to bed, you filthy little girl!" she yelled again, purposely stomping as she walked around the corner to the patio door to let her daughter know that she was serious.

As she turned the corner, she could see the backyard through the door window, and she slowed a little. The low light of evening turned the green paint on the wall odd colors, making them eerie. Picture frames and open closet doors cast long shadows, making dark corners that seemed to taunt Macy, as if the darkness knew something that she did not.

Her face went completely white as she peered out into the peacefulness outside. It was calm and tranquil. The only sound was that of the breeze, and the only movement was that of the swaying, flapping grass.

She didn't have to look to be sure, but she did anyway. Deep in the pit of her gut, she knew before she'd even called out her child's name. But she opened the door and looked outside, and heard the most horrifying sound she'd ever heard: nothing. No sound of her child laughing, or playing in the mud, or chasing leaves. Not a giggle, or a whine, or even a scream.

She ran out into the yard, and started to look around, tiny pebbles digging into the soles of her feet and drawing blood, not that she cared. She pushed back the tree leaves, hoping to find something. Any trace of her little angel, but there was nothing. Just trees so old that they creaked, their branches hanging low, as if in sorrow.

"George!" Macy called, spinning around and running back into the house. "George, it's Kerri!"

ʎ‸ʎ

Mike and Cathy walked down Lee Street hand in hand. As late evening hit, the stars sparkled dimly in the sky, just waiting for the sun to go to bed so that they could play.

The sidewalk was well-lit by the street lamps that loomed above the lovers on huge, towering poles. The city had put more and more of them up lately, trying to keep the streets as illuminated as possible. They said it was to make people feel safe, but they knew full well that they were only doing it to appease the journalists and the little old ladies who had rioted for something to be done. Electricity for bulbs is cheaper than a competent police force, after all.

More leaves had gathered, mobbing the streets and throwing themselves against anyone who dared walk by, as if they'd taken over. The leaves added a voice to the wind. The cold chill could no longer sneak up on you and send shivers down your spine, making you flinch. Now you could see it coming because of the leaves it wore, and zip your jacket up to near-strangling levels before it caught you. Sometimes, the gusts would even turn away if they knew you saw them, spinning around in tiny tornados filled with grit and sand, until flying off in another direction.

In any event, the walk of the two lovers was not quelled by the winds, only propelled by them. As they stepped over the leaves, they made crunching sounds like potato chips until they were kicked away by their heels, forced back onto the wind again.

The sky was a tapestry of blues and purples and yellows. If they thought it was strange that the sun made its most glorious appearances just before it went to sleep, Mike and Cathy were appreciating it too much to pay it heed.

Somewhere, somebody played music far too loudly, but here it was just a soft whisper; a beat for the two to walk to. Their strides were so unified, so in tune with one another, that a casual onlooker would have thought they were dancing, their bodies swaying to beats and chimes that only they could hear.

The scent of overcooked steaks wafted toward them, tickling their tastebuds while, unbeknownst to them, a middle-aged man cursed loudly as he tried in vain to put out the fire that had erupted from his barbeque.

His hands felt warm inside of hers, and although the freezing air had taken the rest of his body to sub-zero temperatures, Mike could not do anything to suppress the growing smile on his face. Nor did he want to, because the warmth from her hand had somehow made its way to his heart, and he found himself greeting everyone he passed with a smile and a nod. He looked at her, smiling as he never had, and found it was reciprocated in kind, if not better. "How do you do?" he said in a muddled British accent, making an over-exaggerated bow at an elderly woman. The old biddy stopped and looked him up and down, no doubt wondering how he managed to hide his eighteen other heads under that shirt, then clutched her purse and scuttled away.

Cathy tried to contain her laughter, but found that it was like trying to contain a dam by plugging it with a finger. Soon it flowed out of her, and she slapped Mike playfully on the arm to get him to stop. "You're awful!" she proclaimed, still laughing.

"And you love me," Mike shot back, tapping her lightly on the nose to annunciate his point.

"True," Cathy admitted without pause.

"You loooove me!" Mike sang, thrusting his hands into the air and making a long 'o' sound, like an opera singer.

"Yes, I do," Cathy whispered.

"*You,*" Mike gasped, grabbing her quickly by the waist and pulling her into him and tilting his chin down until he looked like an old man with thirteen chins, "*love* me."

"Incredibly," she assured him, giving him a wide-eyed stare that meant she knew people were watching. "Now can we stop it, please, now, stop it?" she begged, tapping him on both shoulders to signal him to let her go.

"Somebody, stop me!" he yelled, doing an impression of Jim Carrey in *The Mask* while waving one arm around gracefully and holding her hand with the other, spinning her toward him as though they were waltzing. "It had to be you..." he started to sing, softly at first and then raising his voice so that anyone could hear them. "It had to be youuuu..."

"Okay, Mike, you have to stop now."

"Looking around, finally found..."

"Really, you can give it up."

He dipped her suddenly, kissing her passionately, his tongue slipping against hers for the briefest of moments. "Somebody whoooo..."

"You sound like an owl," she remarked dryly.

He hoisted her back onto her feet in an instant, sending her spinning until he grabbed her hand, snapping them both back into place. "I'm sorry, I know you were talking, but I was distracted. All I could think about is that fact that..." he ran at her, leaping into her arms until they both fell down on the grass behind them. "...You love me."

"More than anything," she laughed, kissing him on the nose. "But why are you acting like this?"

"Hmm," Mike hummed. He looked thoughtful, or at least pretended to, bringing a finger to his head and scratching it methodically. "Why am I acting this way? Hmmm, that's a tough one, you know? I wonder..." He turned, looking into a restaurant across the road from them, where a bearded, overweight man sat down and ate. "Let's ask this guy."

"Mike, no!" Cathy squealed, trying to grab his arm, but he shrugged her off joyfully and just walked on in. She ran after him.

"You!" Mike yelled menacingly, pointing to the man just as he stuffed his mouth full of sandwich. "I wanna ask you something, and you better pray you get the answer right..." he glared as the man swallowed hard, looking up with fear. "Why am I acting this way?"

The man gulped down the rest of his food. "I dunno, man!" he yelled incoherently, peppers falling out of his mouth and rolling down his shirt, staining it.

"See?" Mike yelled, throwing his hands into the air as he rushed Cathy back out the door. "He doesn't know either! Maybe it's because there's a full moon out tonight. Maybe it's because I can see it reflecting off of your eyes as the grass and leaves dance around you but never touch you. Maybe because of the way your hair catches in the wind and then falls perfectly back into place like nothing happened." He smiled, caressing her face. "Maybe it's because of the way your skin feels or the way your cheeks move when you're happy. Maybe it's because you argue with me, even when you know I'm right. Maybe it's because you hit me and think it'll hurt, or because you always feel so bad and kiss it better when it does. Maybe it's because of the way you smell, or the way you taste, or the way your laugh sounds when I've told a really stupid joke and you're the only one who's laughing. Maybe it's because of the way we fight, then promise never to again, then do it again. Maybe it's because you dance in your seat when a good song comes on over the car radio. Maybe it's because you ask me trick questions, ones you know I can't answer. Maybe it's because you think you're fat, when we both know I think you're the most wonderful creature on the face of the planet." He went to her, wrapping his arms around her. "Or maybe it's because you fit perfectly in my arms every time." He kissed her again, passionately, for just a moment, leaving her longing for more.

"Mike," she said after a moment, waiting for the fog that always seemed to cloud her mind when he kissed her to clear, "you're acting crazy."

"Yeah," he agreed, nodding, "that's how people in love act." He kissed her again, then took her hand and started to walk with her. "Come on, it's not much farther."

"Where are we going?"

He smiled. "Shall we ask that guy again?"

ʎ⟨ʎ

"Kerri!" called a Search and Rescue officer off in the distance, as he pushed a mound of shrub aside with such force that it broke at the root.

Every able man in town had come out with George Walker to help search for his little girl in the forest with, while the women stayed home with Macy and the police asked lots of questions. Old man Harper from two houses down had heeded the call so fast that he was only in his long-johns. His wife's striped, flowery slippers flip-flopped on his feet as he ran past trees, his legs getting sliced by branches and thorns.

Terrence's eyes searched back and forth, and even up and down. He was panicking, looking in places that the child could never have set a foot, even turning over medium-sized rocks to make sure she wasn't under them and pushing apart small shrubs. Sweat poured down his brow as he thought of how he'd seen the child play by the road or in the mud, the last bit of innocence left in this town. The last hope for something better to come. "Kerri Walker!" he yelled, climbing a few feet into a tree, trying to see over the undergrowth, trying to see some glimpse of her, just playing in the grass by some clearing.

Chad's face scrunched up as he took off his glasses, trying to see through the darkness a little better. Many of them, like Chad, did not have flashlights, and didn't care. If they got lost, it would only give them an excuse to keep looking; keep searching for the child -- keep searching for hope. Suddenly, a woeful scream sliced through the darkness, and Chad turned abruptly, his long blonde hair discarding the twigs that had become caught in it as he rushed over a stone pile to where the anguished sound had come from.

There, George Walker knelt in a small pile of oddly colored muck. It was only when one got very close that one realized that the mud had been mixed with blood. Not much, but enough to change the color. There, the father of the missing child wept uncontrollably, stopping only long enough to let another wail pass through his lips, as he clutched one small, red, sparkly shoe. It was dimmed only a little by the blood.

In that instant, all men present, no matter what religion they believed in—if any—took off their hats and bowed their heads in prayer, left with a hollow understanding that their prayers might not be answered.

"Oh, Mike," Cathy gasped, as he dramatically opened the front door to a tiny deli on the corner of Fifth Street, motioning for her to enter first. She bowed back to him, feeling silly, as she got into the spirit that he was trying to portray.

"Do you remember?" Mike asked, smiling from ear to ear.

She turned, raising an eyebrow at him. "I couldn't forget if I wanted to."

"Do you?"

"Only when I'm with my other boyfriend."

"Huh?" he spat quickly, his face going white.

She giggled at him, and then he began to laugh a little too, remembering every laugh they'd had through the years.

"Where are they?" Cathy said impatiently, blowing a strand of hair out of her face.

Mike sat across from her, wondering the same thing. "I don't know," he admitted. "I hope they show up soon."

Cathy huffed. "They better."

Mike raised an eyebrow. "But it wouldn't be so bad if it were just the two of us... would it?"

Cathy glanced from her salad to Mike. He was looking straight into her eyes. She'd never seen him look at her that way before. But, to be fair, she couldn't recall ever looking at him that way before either. They both leaned in and kissed. The second their lips met, they both pulled back, a little afraid. They leaned in again, and held it longer this time.

"It was Sara's, wasn't it?" Cathy asked, trying hard to remember as they sat down in the same booth they had a lifetime ago.

Mike nodded, "Yep. She told you to be here, and she

got Xander to tell me the same."

"Remember how we thought at first that maybe they'd gotten together, and that's why they hadn't shown?"

He laughed as he poured himself a coffee and took a sip. "Yeah, wishful thinking, huh?"

"I dunno. I like to think that if they'd had more time..."

"Me too," Mike agreed, nodding. "And I'll always be grateful that we didn't wait until it was too late, like poor Xander."

"I know, this has got to be killing him."

"It is," Mike responded, sighing. "He won't say it, but I know. It's obvious. How could it not be? Today is the three month anniversary of Sara's death, for gawd's sake."

"It's the three month anniversary of a lot of things," Cathy mumbled glumly, pressing a hand against her pelvis gently.

Mike frowned, deciding to change the subject. "Remember the time Sara hooked up with that Canadian kid, Keenan, on a dare?"

Suddenly she erupted with laughter, her woes from a moment ago fading away. "How could he not have realized? The kid was like, three feet tall, and if he'd popped all of his zits then he would have lost half of his face!"

"One thing about Sara, she never backed down from anything. She always did what she wanted, when she wanted," Mike added.

"Yeah," Cathy smirked, "She really used the expression 'seize the moment' to death, didn't she?"

Mike shrugged. "I dunno. I like to think that she did

everything she wanted to before she died. She definitely wouldn't have had any regrets. Sometimes I wish I could be like that, especially now that--"

"Hey hey!" came a high-pitched, annoying voice from the entrance to the deli, the small bell above it ringing loudly as the Peterson girls walked in, their smiles wide and stupid enough not to realize the moment that they'd interrupted.

Julie wore a short black skirt with a black leather jacket, completely inappropriate for this or any other time of year. Her lips had been painted a dark red that was almost black, her eyelids a dark blue. Her face was covered in makeup to hide the freckles that she despised with a passion, giving her skin a milky quality. Her brown hair was messed up from the wind, making her look as wild as she often felt. Her emerald eyes sparkled and shone, looking at Mike and Cathy from behind her toothy grin.

Mandy walked in behind her, without the wide smile. Her short brown hair was tied up in a stubby ponytail, revealing the small, m-shaped scar on her forehead. Her face looked different than usual, and it took Mike and Cathy a moment to realize that she wasn't wearing any makeup, not even lipstick. She wore a sweater that was far too big for her, a plain dark-blue in color, except for her name across the sleeve in white. She wore denim overalls, the top part of which were covered by the sweater, making the bottom look baggy. They were paint-splattered. Her eyes were mostly glued to the ground, careful to make contact with neither Mike nor Cathy. Especially not Cathy.

"Hi guys, how are you doing?" Julie said, dancing across the floor and plopping down next to Mike, grabbing his coffee and taking a sip, then spitting it back into the cup. "Ew, who drinks black? What are you, some kinda caffeine addict or something? Ugh. Anyway, what's up?"

"We're having some time *alone*," Mike stressed, nudging Julie away from him.

"Well, that's over, now. We'll stay with you."

Mandy still stood by the door, not speaking, and looking very much like a wall flower.

Cathy frowned at her, knowingly.

"What are you doing here, Julie?" Mike asked finally, sighing heavily.

"Just out looking for Xander. Do you know where he is?"

"Probably at the cemetery," Cathy breathed.

"Why would he go somewhere like that?"

"To pay his respects. It was three months ago today that Sara died."

Julie's face went even whiter, and for once it seemed as though she had nothing to say. "Come on, Mandy," she said, grabbing the girl by the sleeve. "I'm taking you home."

Before she was hauled out the door, Mandy shot a look at Mike. A smile, and then a wink, followed finally by a nod.

Both Mike and Cathy sighed, then chuckled a little.

"They certainly do make life interesting, don't they?" Mike coughed, lying back against the booth.

"Never a dull moment," Cathy responded coyly, giving him a mischievous smile as she slid from her side of the booth over to where he sat, placing a hand on the inside of his leg and rubbing it slowly, tenderly. She leaned in and started kissing his neck, causing him to laugh nervously.

"What are you doing?" he asked, trying to say it in a way as to not discourage her from the act.

She smiled, gazing deeply into his eyes. "Seizing the moment," she whispered, leaning in to kiss him gently on the lips.

"They have no idea where she is," Officer Moony cursed, turning toward Constable Lyle as they both stared into the wooded area behind the Walkers' house, scratching their heads. "They found a shoe and some blood. We can give it to the dogs with some clothes and try to get her back here as soon as possible. Did you call the dogs?"

"For the third time, I called the dogs," Lyle responded, frowning. "They're coming as fast as they can."

"That might not be fast enough. Every second this girl is gone is another second the kidnapper has with her: not something I'm overly comfortable with."

"I know. The parents are hick morons. Didn't even thin out the forest and put up a fence. That kid could have been murdered ten feet from their back door and they wouldn't have seen it."

"Don't say that word. It won't be long before the media gets hold of this, and you don't wanna slip up like that and send the mother to the loony bin."

"The media here are stupid. I wish White were still here. He'd have this solved by now."

"Tell me about it."

"You gotta wonder, though. Town like this, how does someone justify leaving their kids unattended?"

"They've lived in that house for ten years, without incident. Not even a yell late at night. People think that if something doesn't happen for long enough that it never will."

There was a long silence between the both of them then, their swollen stomachs growling for food even as they forced down egg salad sandwiches.

"Do you think she's alive?" Moony asked, his ears wanting to hear something he knew he wouldn't.

Lyle sighed. "I don't know. I don't believe in miracles."

The graveyard was a still, lonely place in the first few hours of night, with nothing but a constant, slow howl to let you know that you haven't gone completely deaf. It was an atmosphere that Xander was used to. The cold chill of nightfall had become like a second home to him. It was the only time he knew real peace.

All around him were the graves of his friends, the nearest and dearest to his heart. But the one at the top of the hill, the one he stood at now, was closer than all the rest of them combined. Her name, in life, had been Sara Johnson, the greatest love he'd ever known in his short time on this earth, until she was taken from him. Ripped. Pulled away from him by a monster the likes of which the world had never known.

"Remember your funeral, Sara?" he asked shyly with an embittered lip as he stared down the headstone, cracking his knuckles before reaching into his breast pocket, pulling out a smoke and then lighting it, taking a long drag. "Right before I made the vow to protect and all that? It was a nice day. I thought it was gonna rain. It always rains in comic books when they have funerals, y'know? You used to hate it when I read comics... not as much as you hated it when I read school books, though, huh?" He laughed, resting the cigarette between his lips. "Anyway, remember I was supposed to read your eulogy, but I couldn't? Well, it's taken a few months, but I think I finally figured out what I needed to say." He took a deep breath, his chest heaving. He began to read, his voice uneven and unnatural as he read his own words.

"I don't understand. I don't understand this world, and they keep telling me that I have to. They keep throwing these things at me, like I'm supposed to save the world or something, when really it's all I can do to keep from crying from minute to minute, and I want to know how you did it. How did you crawl through the dirt and the grime and come out clean on the other side? How did you stay so pure? Out of everything, that's the one thing I can't manage without you, Sara. The loneliness I can handle. Even the pain, most of the time, but I need you to finish telling me how to live without you. How to live this life that you helped me make..."

Tears started rolling down his cheeks, but he sucked them back, trying to keep his composure.

"Every night, I try to make you proud of me. I try to make the world a better place, but there's always a price. It can never be a complete win. I put Derek away after he went on a killing spree under my nose for a month. I put

Phillips away after he scarred Cathy. I defeated Genblade after he killed an innocent lawyer. I defeated a gang of Tee's only to have one of them shoot Sud. The only exception to the rule is Blackheart, and that's just because she beat me completely. And you, Sara... why is it I'm never the one who pays the price for my failures?"

Kerri cried more as she lost her second shoe, the branches scraping at exposed flesh.

"Why is it that it's always those closest to me, or worse yet, complete innocents, that get hurt when I can't cut it?"

The sounds of the demon's grunts overwhelmed her, drowning out the low whimper that had been emanating from her throat since the creature had snatched her from her peaceful backyard.

Xander knelt down before the grave, feeling the cold earth through his black jeans. "But most of all, I have to know why it was you. Why you had to leave me here. It's like you took all of the air out of my world, and now I'm stuck suffocating in this vacuum. . Is that my life, now? Spending every waking moment just waiting for death so I might be with you again?" He frowned, shaking his head. "I'm sorry Sara, but I can't live like that. I can't. I have to hope that tomorrow will be better, but I also have to know that it won't be. That it can't be. Because you're not going to crawl out of all that dirt and soil and be pure again for me, are you?"

He frowned, caressing the grass and pretending it was her hair.

"I've met someone," he blurted, then turned red with embarrassment. "There, I said it. I wasn't hiding it from you, just myself, really. She's not really my type... but then, I guess since I've never had a girlfriend I don't really have a *type*," he laughed, tossing his smoke away and curling his fingers into the dirt nervously. "Just like when you were alive, I have to admit things to you before I can admit them to myself. She's not you, though. She could never be you. She's a little like you, though. She's definitely got your forwardness with men, not that I ever saw any of that from you. She's not as kind as you," he smiled, "and she has all the grace and tact of a water buffalo with a hernia, but she's good to me. And she cares about me. And... I think I'm ready to start caring about her." He laughed a little. "This wasn't much of a eulogy. But, I think it was mostly about putting you to rest, and it was long overdue. I've been keeping you alive in my heart for so long... this is the first time it's occurred to me that maybe you wanted some sleep." He bowed his head for a moment in prayer. He stayed there for a long time, just feeling the wind and listening to the sounds around him.

"Can I help you with something?" he asked the person who approached him from behind. He had known who it was just from the scent, and the way she stomped of leaves making her way up the gentle slope of the hill.

He grinned a little. "Hello, Julie."

"Am I interrupting something?" she panted slightly, catching her breath and trying to get her wind-ruffled hair out of her face.

"Not really. I just wanted to be alone," he replied, turning back toward the grave.

"Oh," Julie sighed, turning to look back down the hill. "And, away we go again..." she said, rolling her eyes as she started back down the hill.

"No, that's all right," Xander chuckled, motioning her to come stand next to him. "I can be alone with you here."

She smiled, stepping up to stand next to him. He stared down at the grave, not moving or speaking. She tried to have the same amount of focus on the slab of stone. She licked her lips, then smacked them together. Then she did it again. She waved her hands back and forth, looking around at the other graves. "Depressing," she mumbled.

"Hmm?" Xander hummed, giving her a look. He was so absorbed in his thoughts, that he almost forgot she was there.

"All the headstones," she elaborated, motioning to the long line of graves. "I dunno. It's probably dumb, but when I die, I want something funny to be put on my urn."

"Urn?"

"Getting cremated," she explained with a smile. "There is way too much, like, prime real estate being taken up by graveyards. I mean, there are, like, so many homeless in New York, couldn't all that land be used for, like, cheap housing or something?"

Sticking his lower lip out, he tilted his head to one side for a second, then nodded. "I guess that's true."

"Damn right."

"Maybe I'll be cremated," he stopped, brushing some dust offthe side of his jacket. "Hey, did you just make a good point?"

"I was overdue," she shrugged comically, rolling her eyes. She looked at him, then knocked on his forehead with one fist. "Doof-head."

"You went from intelligent conversation about homeless shelters to calling me a doof-head."

"Uh-huh!" she chimed, giving him a big smile and flapping her arms against her sides.

"So... you're insane."

"Uh-huh!"

"But you're still Julie?" he asked, quieter now. Almost romantically.

"Uh-huh," she breathed, looking at his lips.

"Good. I can deal with that."

She closed her eyes, leaning in to kiss him. At the last moment, he turned to face the grave, his demeanor solid as stone, as though the conversation had never happened. She sighed, scuffing her feet against the grass and looking around at the different last names on the graves, paying close attention to old friends and people she didn't know with her own last name. She stayed silent for a long time, just observing him as he stood. He looked like a living, breathing painting. *A painting named 'The unmoving man who never ever moved, not even to pee,'* she decided on the spur of the moment, nodding silently at the excellent name.

"So," she said finally, after a great time where nothing had been said. Verbally, anyway. "Anniversary, huh? I get that. A lot of my friends died that night, too. It also makes me think of Derek, and Grendel's party... those entire few weeks of my life. It's not just the date they died, it's like, it's the date that who we were died, y'know? It's like the woolly mammoth. He's just chillin' out one day (pardon the pun), when... BAM!... he's extinct. I doubt he even saw it coming, stupid elephant wannabe. Anyway, that's what it was like. It was like something hit this town, and it was, like, evolve or die. So, some of us died, but some of us had to change to survive. We had to adapt. To, like, evolve. Or, something like that. I think that's what I thought."

All the time that she had been speaking, Xander had not moved or even flinched. It was only because of her close proximity to him that she knew he was actually breathing. Then, suddenly, he raised an eyebrow and turned to look at her. "What?" he asked loudly, completely perplexed.

"Sorry," she apologized, genuinely. "I rambled. I was talking about this being the three-month anniversary of Sara's death and all."

"Hmm," Xander huffed, then turned back to the grave.

"What? Did I do something wrong again?" she pleaded, grabbing him by the arm and turning him toward her.

"No," he shrugged. "I just hadn't realized this was the anniversary."

"Then why are you here?"

He turned back to the grave, hands at his sides. "I do this every night."

She stood there with him for another thirty minutes. The wind picked up, and her hand started to get cold. It lingered near his hand, so she took it without question or pause. She clasped his hand so tightly that she made impressions in his skin, and he enjoyed every second of it.

He smiled, nodding down at Sara's grave. "Yeah, yeah," he said sarcastically. "I know. She's great, isn't she?"

He felt the heat coming off of her skin, even as he looked into her eyes. They sparkled in the dim moonlight, alive with fear and excitement all at the same time. Their skin twitched and tugged as they touched, feeling the warmth emanating from each other.

They kissed, and if there was any uncertainty, neither of them thought to notice.

The skin on her stomach was smooth and milky white, without wrinkle or blemish. There were stretch lines around her waist and breasts, which he noticed as her shirt fell to the floor a few moments ago.

For a moment, he was on top of her.

Uncertain, she withdrew.

"..ure?

"You sure?"

They both nodded. They had both asked.

He stroked her cheek with his thumb as he kissed her, her tongue moving quickly inside of his mouth. Every taste,

every sensation,

a new surprise.

Every touch, every time she felt his body close to hers, she would pull away from shock, then immediately go looking for the same spot again, only to find something better.

His hand drifted down from her cheek, down her neck. He stopped at her breasts, tracing the red marks that came with her age and their growth. She laughed, but was embarrassed.

She is beautiful, he thought.

She *is* beautiful.

His lips followed his hands, caressing her. He breathed deeply as the taste excited him further, pulling their bodies closer.

She stiffened, uncertain, but never wanting him to
                          stop.

He looked up every few seconds, unsure himself. Making sure that she was okay, and briefly kissing her lips before continuing his descent.

He was tracing her naval with one finger.

Am I fat?

She is beautiful, he thought, unable to think anything else.

She *is* beautiful.

His fingers went down then, and electricity surged through her body.

Twitch.

Her leg twitched, and again, she was embarrassed.

The embarrassment was still not enough to get it to
                          stop.

twitching.

Again, his tongue followed his fingers, as they went

even lower still.

Soft.

There was the pressure of resistance, a sudden rush of pain, and then it was a rush again.

Like sour limes.

Her body welcomed him, wrapping her legs around him,

Tender.

pulling him in further.

Moist.

Beautiful, he thought, the word screaming at him everywhere he looked.

Wet.

Beautiful.

lime.

he was on her again, but this time she made no effort to

stop.

Him, wrapping her legs around and kissing his passionately as he sank into her, for his first time. Her first time. Their first time.

His head flew back so hard that he thought it might snap his neck, his brain exploding with pleasure from mere contact.

He melted into her.

Sank into her.

Soft

Lime

Tender

Moist

Wet

Her back arched, and he went deeper still.

Suddenly, it was okay for her to move. It came naturally. She did not want to

stop.

energy built up inside her and everything started to get faster more alert things stopped making sense as the world began to spin around her making her dizzy at first then the feeling began to build it was almost like she needed to pee but she did not she felt herself filling up creating pressure wanted to release it wanting it to come out come out went harder tried to make it slow down no rush but she wanted it to come to come so badly she could almost taste it

lime

suddenly the feeling spread traveling from the soft lime tender moist wet warm and going up her spine in tremendous leaps and bounds

"Don't."

stop.

The en-er-gy kept build-ing and get-ting more pow-er-ful with ev-er-y step it took then it ex-plo-ded out of the back of her skull like fire-works and misted down over her body, a calmed and relaxed feeling spreading over her. She smiled.

His eyes grew wide as he went faster, harder... then

stopped, exploding himself. It felt like she was pulling back as he became soft and small, humbled by what they had accomplished.

Slowly, as one, their breathing became normal again. The world stopped spinning out of control, and they relaxed in one another's arms.

"I love you, Cathy."

"I love you, Mike."

They kissed passionately.

lime.

stop.

∧‹∧›

Alone at home, Mandy watched *The Late Show* on her tiny, fuzzy television, waiting for the host to say something funny. He did not, but everyone seemed to laugh anyway. She looked at her watch, wondering how long it would be until one of those other late-night shows with the stupid stories and the really bad, naked actors would come on. It would be at least another half hour, a million light-years away for one with an attention span so small.

She sighed, looking around her room for something to do.

It was bare, and just a little bit dark. Everything looked different now. The light from the television was all that kept the room from being pitch black, and even its glow had its limits. She could not see the corners of her small, claustrophobic attic room, and the television made cruel shadows that moved and whispered in the dark.

A shiver ran down her spine that had nothing to do with the cold.

She had left all her things with her mother in Coral Cove when Auntie Sam made her move out here with Julie. All her friends and everything she had was back in that town, but she was here in this one.

Keeping both eyes on the darkness to make sure nothing jumped out at her, she reached under her bed and pulled out a small, furry notebook with a lock that always had its key in it. She turned the elaborately designed key and opened the diary. Notes that she had passed back and forth between friends tumbled out from between pages, and she tucked them away behind the back cover before flipping through to find her place.

June - Mom's drunk again. I tried to talk to her about a boy at school, but she just yelled about Dad...

July - I went all the way with Tom, then yesterday I heard him telling his friends how easy I was... saw him kissing Anna Speads.

September - Why does he have to hurt me when he

October - I don't deserve to live... stupid h...

November - I know something. Something so weird and awful that it could probably get me killed. I've never been more scared, or excited.

She stopped, pulling out the pen she'd won at one of those dime-a-dozen amusement parks that travel around the interstate and continued the passage, a sly smirk on her face.

Bad men took me. They took me away. I didn't think this place was any better than home, but then he came. He's so smart, and so strong. He stopped all of the bad men, dragged them off into the darkness. I thought he killed them, but he didn't. He saved me, though. Saved me from all of them, like a guardian angel.

He was black -- not African-American black, real black. Shadow black -- with red eyes. They were gentle, though. I didn't think red eyes could be gentle, but he looked at me, and then they were. Big, red eyes... that were kinda pointy. They were round, but they turned up. Like a cat's eyes, a little.

He had so many muscles, and he just threw the bad guys around like they were nothing. It was great.

He had claws. Claws like a bird. An eagle. Angels have bird wings, so why not claws, I guess? He needed something to save me, so I guess he grew them.

I think he had wings, but I'm not sure. They could have been folded back. I think he had wings.

My own guardian angel. A black angel sent to make every-thing better.

I've got a secret.

I know who the Black Angel really is...

Mandy giggled to herself, smiling as she continued to write.

ᚠᚣᚱ

She'd stopped crying.

She still wanted to, it was just that the tears wouldn't come anymore. Still, Kerri Walker sat in a field about twenty kilometers from her house, deep inside the for-est. The air stung at the cuts and bruises all over her. She thought about running, but every time she did, she no-ticed the bones of a small dog lying near her, and decided not to.

Blood vessels had ruptured in her right eye, mak-ing her perfect face look torn, like a used piece of paper. Where smiles had once been, now there was only a blank expression. She had stopped crying after the first few hours, when neither the creature nor anyone else had paid much attention to it. Her clothes were muddy and dirty, with twigs stuck in them and rips everywhere.

Once, while the beast was dragging her away, she

thought she heard her mother cry out to her, but she couldn't summon her voice to call back.

Now, the monster was hunched into a ball about ten feet from where she sat, using its massive, knife-like claws to dig at the soil, shredding grass and placing it into a small pile that was beginning to look like the bed her hamster used to make for herself before she went to hamster heaven.

Kerri felt the tears begin again as she thought of her mom and her dad. A small whimper escaped from her lips, and the tears rolled down her cheeks.

The creature looked up, stiff but alert, like a horse that had heard a strange noise. It sniffed the air twice, then turned toward her suddenly, as if only just noticing that she was there. It growled deep in its throat.

It leapt toward her, using one of its massive hands to pin her to the ground, digging its claws into the ground to keep her there. Slivers branched off of its body, moving about it like tentacles. Teeth-like spikes sprouted at the end of each, and they reached out toward her, ripping and shredding at her.

It climbed onto her.

She screamed in pain at first, just as her body found its tears. The creature clawed her across the face savagely, and her screams immediately stopped, quieting to a low whimper.

The whimper would have been heard long into the night, had anyone been around to hear it.

CHAPTER FOUR:
GHOSTS

Friday, Day Three

"So, what do you think about this young Kerri girl?" asked O'Toole, clicking the top of his retractable pen and writing the date across the top of his notepad, which was completely hidden behind the flaps of Xander's folder.

Xander glared at O'Toole, biting his tongue. He avoided the doctor's gaze, instead looking all around the room at the various university degrees and souvenirs that lined the walls and shelves around the office. He pointed one out, smiling. "Hey, you never told me you met President Bush."

O'Toole smiled, leaning over to glance at his own photo. "Yes. Remarkable man, really."

"That's kind of ironic."

"Oh?"

"Yeah," Xander said, his smile wiping away to become deadly serious. "Because, you know, you've got all the tact of carpet bombing."

O'Toole sighed, putting down the pen. He looked

down, then brought his face back up. For the first time, the man was showing the stress he must feel every day, making Xander pity him. The doctor got out from behind his desk, leaving the file, and came over to sit next to him. "Sorry," he said honestly, resting the heel of one foot against the knee of the other leg. "Tell you what? No more recording everything you say. We'll just... talk."

Xander squinted, slowly nodding.

By this time, everyone in town knew about what had happened to Kerri Walker. Snatched from her own home. The child had never even been outside of the town limits, and rarely out of her parents' sight. Xander couldn't help think of how terrified she must be, how alone she must feel.

He was also barely able to keep his claws from un-sheathing as he thought about what he'd do when he found the sick bastard that had done this.

"Really, Alexander," O'Toole said, snapping Drew out of his murderous fantasy. He took off one shoe and started to casually rub his own foot, wearing a facial expression that greatly resembled ecstasy. "What are you thinking about right now?"

"Killing a person."

Silence.

O'Toole swallowed hard, taking a glance back at his pen and paper and fighting the urge to dive at it. "Really? Who?"

"I dunno. Could be anyone."

"I s-see..." he stammered, again wishing for his note-pad.

"I just want to find the bastard who did this to a little

girl and claw their eyes out," he grunted, pretending to strangle an invisible foe.

O'Toole sighed in relief. "Oh. Yes, Alexander, I'm sure we all feel like that. But what can we really do about it?"

"I dunno. Anything's better than this. I should be helping."

"What do you think you can do to help?"

Xander was about to answer, then stopped himself. "I dunno."

"How have you been sleeping?" O'Toole asked suddenly, pulling a one-eighty on their topic.

Xander stared for a minute, leaning back, stroking his upper lip before pointing at the doctor. "Do you hear voices?"

"Now, what makes that question so hard to answer?"

"No, seriously. Cause, I'm kinda hungry, and I'm really broke. I figure if I turn you in, I can get myself fifty bucks and a fruit basket. Wadda-ya say? Gonna help a guy out?"

"Okay, I think that's taking it a bit far. But, now that you mention it, I'm a bit peckish, too,"O'Toole added.

"You can eat my ass."

"Eat your ass?" O'Toole exclaimed, eyes wide. He pointed a finger at the boy. "Listen here, you..."

"Jeez, what is it with you people and molesting your patients?" Xander laughed, shrugging and looking around at the fake studio audience that he was sure would have been in stitches by now. "First you talk about sleeping with me, now you're ordering me to eat your ass. Explain yourself!"

O'Toole sighed, laying his head against his desk and

looking catatonic for a moment. "Just answer the question, dammit."

"Language."

"Shut up."

"Why do you want to know how I'm sleeping?" Xander asked finally, raising an eyebrow. "To complete your mental fantasy?"

"No," Warren replied, regaining his composure. "It's part of my study. People under hypnosis tend to change their sleep patterns sporadically. I don't want an upset sleep pattern to upset your day-to-day routine."

"Oh," Xander huffed, puffing put his cheeks and thinking, trying to recall the night before. "No, I slept all right," Xander smiled, realizing that he actually had.

"Good."

"Yeah."

"So, getting back on subject, did you have anything to do with the disappearance of Kerri Walker?" Warren said calmly, all in one breath as to get it out as soon as possible.

Xander felt the smile fade from his face, and his claws were ready to pop again. Another instant and he might have transformed right then and there.

"Did you kidnap her to fulfill some sexual or psychological need you might have?"

The boy's nostrils flared, and he thought he might soon discover that he also had the power to breathe fire. "Excuse me?"

"Did you do it to prove yourself to the gang that was responsible for the recent deaths of youth in town?"

"The Tees."

"Yes, the Tees," O'Toole nodded. "Sorry, I couldn't recall without my notes."

"I have nothing to do with them, aside from the fact that I would burn each of them alive if they had something to do with this."

"Really? Thomas Drake thought you were involved with them," O'Toole pointed out, putting his show back on. "Carl Dent too. I'd sure like to ask them what their thoughts are on all this... but they're dead."

"That's not my fault," Xander stressed between gritted teeth.

"Did she feel good, Xander?"

"Shut up!" Xander yelled, his voice completely that of the womb, a low, guttural sound. He pulled back, trying to restrain himself, although part of him did not want to. He got up and grabbed his book bag, heading toward the door. "See ya around, Tool."

"I'm sorry, Xander," Warren said sincerely.

Xander turned and looked at the man. His head was down and his shoulders slumped to the floor, bringing the tall man down a peg or two.

"I truly am. But, if I find out that you or any other of my patients were involved in this... doctor-patient privilege be damned. I will hang you myself."

Xander nodded, turning back to the exit and closing the door behind him.

When the door snapped shut, Warren O'Toole smirked to himself, reaching into his pocket and pulling out a miniature tape recorder, pressing a button to make it stop recording. He scurried back to his desk to begin transcribing, pressing play.

"Shut up!" Xander's voice rang out, filled with static on the recorder. O'Toole raised an eyebrow, then began playing the clip over and over again.

Xander stormed down the hallway, his book bag slung over his back carelessly. He was walking like an army cadet, or a storm trooper, like he had some purpose. He stopped at his locker, turning the dial to 19 - 08 - 04, then opened it, throwing his bag in with a clang. He slammed the door with such force that it bounced back and nudged him, so he punched it as hard as he could, screamed angrily, then turned and started walking again.

Immediately, he bumped into Julie.

"Hi!" she chimed, waving as if to get his attention, even though they were the only two people in the hallway. "Yeah, I hate those lockers too. This school is so cheap, they really should get new ones. So, about last night, I'm sorry if I was, like, bugging you or something," she pulled back her hair and avoided making eye contact, "but, like, if you enjoyed yourself as much as I did, then I'm not sorry, because I, like, really enjoyed myself and stuff, and I was wondering..."

Xander rolled his eyes, turning to look directly at her. "Julie," he snapped, rudely flicking her on the forehead with one finger.

"Ow," she whined, rubbing it for a second, then smiling at him again. "Yeah?"

"I don't have time," he grunted, bumping past her as though she wasn't even there.

As he turned the corner to walk away from her, her

lower lip stuck out. She sat on the floor, leaning up against his locker. Anyone that saw her was reminded of the agonized cries of another little girl in Coral Beach right now, and they shook their heads in dismay.

Chad stopped for a moment when he reached a large field, resting against the great stick he'd been using to help prop himself up. Sweat was pouring down his brow now, and his lungs ached. He needed a cigar, but he smoked his last one about three hours before.

It was starting to get cold out now, and beads of sweat were freezing onto his forehead, making him wish that he hadn't abandoned his trench coat along the trail a few miles back.

Letting out a long, hard breath, he scanned the field. It was starting to get dark, and he was miles from the nearest road. This would be his second day not showing up at the office, but since his supervisor was out searching too, he doubted that anyone would mind. His eyes darted over the horizon. It looked almost peaceful, like a Da Vinci landscape, with golden rays from the sun caught in the tall yellow grass.

Then, something caught his eye: a blue piece of fabric caught in an alder branch near the center of the field. Letting his stick fall to the ground, he walked over to it and carefully picked it up.

"Oh, no," he frowned, as he held little Kerri's dress, ripped and stained with blood. Next to it were the bones of a small dog, picked clean of all meat, the eyes rotting in its tiny skull. "Please," he pleaded, gripping the tattered clothing. "Please, God, no."

CHAPTER FIVE:
RETURN

-pit-

-pit pit-

Xander grunted, refusing to open his eyes as he felt the water drip onto his cheek.

His other cheek was already soaked, along with that side of his head, and he had the overpowering taste of dirt in his mouth. Something was wriggling dangerously close to one eye, so he opened it to see what it was.

Immediately, his open eye stung so much that it nearly blinded him. "Argh!" he bellowed as he sat up, realizing that he had been half submerged in a mud puddle. He spat twice, and fair sized rocks came out, along with one tooth from the back of his mouth, followed by some coppery-tasting blood that, mixed with the grime, made him want to vomit.

-pit-

Drops of condensation from the leaves of an overhead tree landed on his clay-matted hair, making it run down into his eye. Blood vessels were opened in both eye sockets, and pebbles stuck into them, making it impossible to see anything straight. He reached up to get them out, promptly screaming in pain.

His claws had still been out, and the action had only served to further gouge his eyes.

"What the fuck?!" he yelled, grabbing a handful of cloudy water and splashing it into his eye, trying to get it to work right again. He opened the other eye, using it to search his surroundings. It was foggy, and he was in the forest. He strained his ears to try and hear which direction traffic was in to get his bearings. He found he heard none at all, meaning he was further out than the womb would have brought him frivolously.

His breathing was labored, and when he looked down there was a large branch sticking out of him, with blood-soaked leaves still hanging on one end. His eyes went wide, and suddenly he could taste the sap on his breath, filtering up from his lungs. Forcing both eyes open despite the pain, which seemed minimal now, he checked himself over.

His kneecap was missing. There was a large steel bolt sticking out of one hip, and all of his ribs had been either bruised, cracked, broken, or in some cases, all three. His heartbeat was erratic, meaning there was likely something wrong there, too. He spat again, and a large chunk from the top of his jaw detached from inside his mouth, plopping onto the ground.

"Fuck," he cursed, but it came out muddled. He leaned out over the puddle he'd nearly drowned in. Half his face was covered in mud, but it stung so hard that the muscle might as well have been bare. He began to wash himself off, and the stinging became more and more unbearable the more pressure he put on himself. When he looked back, he realized why. The muscle *was* bare. Whatever had done this to him had taken the flesh off of half his face.

There was something sticking out of his cheek, and when he reached up to pull it out, he saw that chunks were missing out of his arms: bite marks like a dog would make, only bigger. Broader. He pulled the foreign object from his face and examined it.

It was a tooth.

A long, sharp, tooth.

"What the hell is going on here?" he wondered, looking around to try and get his bearings. There was no noise except for the rustle of curious woodland creatures, but would still not get close. A squirrel, maybe even a chipmunk or two. Definitely a wolf, by the smell of it. But there was another smell, one besides the pine and dung. One that didn't belong.

He felt the pull of the true womb organ as it tried to divert all of its power to Xander's olfactory senses, telling him that he was on the right track. He took a big whiff, and his eyes opened wide. "Concrete, oil... phosphorous?" he frowned, furrowing his brow. "What would that be doing all the way out here?"

He stopped, turning to look around, suddenly realizing where he was. It was all too familiar now. He staggered to his feet, moving to a nearby tree and pushing its great branches aside. There, looming high above him, was the Engen complex.

A fortress of steel and concrete, it was here that he'd

first battled Genblade. Where he'd been crucified and tortured. Where he'd begged for death time and time again. *Why would the womb bring me here*? He thought to himself, as he limped slowly toward the entrance.

The building had been blown apart by his final battle with Alpha, the mad-scientist that had woken up his Other three months ago. The concrete inside was crumbling everywhere, and Xander had to watch every step he took for fear that the floor might cave in under him. The levels went down further than they went up. If he fell, he'd be falling for a long time.

Paint had been chipped off the walls. Steel girders lined the halls, making it so that you could see into the ceiling and beyond in some spots. There was mold everywhere, and the smell of old, wet books in a library had sunk into everything. Animals both large and small had begun using this place for their home, their feces and nests littering the concrete, yet bringing life to the inanimate stone building.

To his far left, just behind a fallen pillar and some slabs of rock, was a large glass window. It was shattered, but not broken; still clear for the most part, simply spider-webbed in many places. A chipmunk scurried about next to it, barely noticing that Xander was even there.

"Hi, Bob," Xander snickered playfully, picking up a small acorn and tossing it toward the creature.

It looked shocked and offended, then grabbed the acorn and scurried through a hole in the glass into the area below.

Xander's eyes followed it into the pile of rubble and sand below the window. Whatever had been in the large, semi-circular room had received the brunt of the damage from the explosion, demolishing the walls and turning most of the ceiling's steel girders into mulch, which was now the home of a small family of birds.

Only after a moment did he realize what this place was.

He turned around slowly, getting a good look at Alpha's control room. The room below him was the arena, the sick place of torture where he'd battled Genblade, been crucified, and been forced to kill Spider.

The control room was more spacious than he imagined it, even more so now that there were holes blasted in it. Even so, he always pictured it being a little snugger. Like a musty old den where Alpha could smoke a pipe, twirl his mustache and practice laughing evilly while watching *Masterpiece Theater*.

Not that he ever had a mustache.

Or an upper lip, for that matter.

Xander turned around, looking at where a bookcase had been. Most of the books were completely burned to a crisp, but a few were only half burned. *Moby Dick, The Many Adventures of Robin Hood, The Bible...* he stopped at one, taking it off the self, smirking a little. It was *The Strange Tale of Dr. Jekyll and Mr. Hyde*, a first edition, nearly destroyed.

Irony, thy name is evil, he mused, placing the book against the side of the shelf.

Immediately, the wood crumbled and turned to dust, and the rest of the case fell down around Xander's ears with a large crash, the books disintegrating into ash and soot.

He winced, closing his eyes as he waited for the dust to settle, his teeth grinding together. "Uh," he started, opening one eye to take a look around, "I didn't do it?"

Then he stopped, opening his other eye and realizing what stood in front of him. The fire damage was worse on the wall where the bookcase had stood. The walls were blackened by flame, except for one perfect square, which was still shiny and metallic and perfect. Raising an eyebrow curiously, even though it stung the exposed flesh of his face, Xander limped toward the square.

Grunting furiously as blood once again forced its way out through his mouth, he leaned against the untouched metal and pushed. Slowly, it went back into the wall inch by inch, then finally he heard a snap and pulled back. The door reached its springs and jolted to one side, revealing a room dimly lit by red light. The loud buzz of a generator was evident now, and it was clear by the numbers that flashed over the computers that there was still a power supply in this section of the complex.

He turned one monitor toward him. It said the words: 'Subject Health Report' across the top, and was updated every three or four seconds. There was an outline of a human body there, with red splotched on its knees, face, lungs, and all over its body. "It's me," he realized after a moment. He raised a talon and made a small scratch on his right arm, then watching a red splotch appear on the mockup's arm. "Must track me the second I come into range," Xander smirked, amused, until he saw the words at the bottom of the screen. "Situation critical. Cease harm on Womb. Near... death?" He looked down at his gut, which could barely contain his intestines beneath a slight layer of translucent skin.

The room kept going. There were more screens, with an outline of both Genblade and Spider. Genblade's was waiting for a signal, while Spider's was permanently an aqua hue. "Red bad, aqua worse," he chuckled. "I knew I should've gotten a patent on that."

He turned to a fourth screen, one that was also waiting for its subject to return to transmission distance. Leaning in and squinting, Xander couldn't help but crack a smile. "Zakron?" He shook his head. "What kind of a name is Zakron for a genetic experiment? Who is this thing anyway? Maybe they made soup. Genetically enhanced soup, and it ran away or something."

"Yes, because that's likely."

Xander turned, thinking that he'd heard a voice. A voice like springtime. When he looked, there was a long row of cylinders. Looking much like clear, round coffins, each one was made of green glass and an odd viscous fluid pooled around it; fluid that did not seem to want to evaporate.

Carefully, Xander bent down and touched the fluid. It was gooey at first, then it soaked into his hand. Immediately, the cuts and scrapes on his arm began to heal. "Sweet," he said, pumping his arm once in celebration. He turned to the steel-grated clear caskets, all lined up in a row. The glass was broken on all of them, each one long ago smashed by the looks of it. Close to twenty years ago, by the looks of the way the fluids around the glass had softened their edges.

He reached over and dusted off a control switchboard which had a locking mechanism for each door. The words

'Darkness Containment Cells' were engraved on top.

He turned back to the cells with new-found appreciation and horror. "This is where they kept the test subjects before and after me. This was destroyed when... when my mother escaped from Engen." He looked down at the fluid again, taking some and rubbing it on his stomach and then watching it heal. "This is the same gunk that kept Alpha alive for all those years after the explosion."

"Can't get anything past you, can we?"

Stepping up, Xander started to walk past the different coffin cells. As he read the names engraved on each one, he could not help but smile vibrantly, as his past became a little clearer for the first time. Red Falcon, Zero, Abel... these had been his father's: those who had come before him so that he could be what he is today.

He stopped, staring for a moment at the next cell. It read Eve, the first name of the woman who would become Spider. It only now dawned upon him that she was killed less than a thirty second walk from where she had been born. These walls were probably all she'd ever known.

He stiffened, becoming aware of what was happening. He turned around, and he was standing face-to-face with Eve Spider.

Instinctively he lashed out, clawing at the visage. Instead of connecting with flesh, he simply slipped through the air and skidded across the floor, which would have hurt if he hadn't landed in the clear goo. He turned quickly. "How?" he demanded frantically, watching her statically fragmented movements as she jumped across the floor. Her motions were not whole... like watching a movie reel with parts missing. One minute she'd be crouching for a leap, the next she landed. The in between was missing. "How are you here?"

"What do you mean, Womb?" Spider asked, *giggling a little in her lovely voice. The voice that could not have originally belonged to someone so cruel, Xander decided. It must have been taken from a sweet, innocent child and placed within her by Alpha, to put off her enemies.*

"You know what I mean!" he accused, rising to his feet and twisting to follow her as she danced around him, while her swords were sheathed behind her back. "You're not real! You're some fever dream I had when O'Toole knocked me under! How are you here now?"

"Hypnotic suggestion maybe?" she laughed, shooting him a look. *"Have you heard nothing I've said?"*

"Yeah, I remember," he scoffed. "'Those that are allies today will betray me tomorrow,' right? You were talking about Derek, then. So what now? Why are you here? To warn me of the big bad that's coming?"

"I am here because you need me to be here," Spider assured him, *unsheathing a sword and swinging it toward him. To his shock, it cut deep into his cheek.*

"What the fuck?" Xander yelled, grabbing at his face as blood streamed down it. "I didn't think you were real."

"You think many things, Womb, but few are correct. And few are incorrect. All that matters is that you assume all, and that is when it will strike. When you assume that you are safe and snug in your bed with the pretty flowers that dance like rainbows and headphones."

Xander gave her a quizzical look, tilting his head to one side. "I can't put my finger on it, but I think you lost me somewhere. Oh, maybe when you started talking crazy. Just a thought."

"You think you know all, but you don't know him," she accused, pointing her sword at him. "And you don't know her. The one who will start it, with the blonde hair and the blue eyes... She'll sing for you, she will. She'll make you dance and shout, but she whispers the truth to me when she's with her children, she does. She whispers that she won't choose you to be her One and only. She'll choose the child instead, and that's when they'll all turn on you."

Xander took a step forward, then nearly collapsed onto the floor. Getting up and literally holding his legs together, he finished the movement. "Ignoring all the other cryptic crap, what do you mean I don't know him? Who him?"

"The one that did this to you, and the one that will do worse to my dear Adam," she said, her voice becoming a wail when she said her lover's voice. "He'll make him like a faucet, hot and cold running blood. And you will not know, for you do not know yourself."

"Wait, what?" Xander jolted, becoming alert. "What was that last bit? What does it matter whether I know myself or not?"

"Because you are fighting yourself, my boy. Because that's all you've ever done. And even with the traitor helping you, you still cannot fight it. And now yourself is coming, along with the traitor and all his little tin men."

"Traitor? What traitor?"

She pushed him, and he landed on his back. She flipped skillfully, and when she landed she was sitting on his chest, smirking at him. "You know what I like best about you genetically altered guys? You're always good for a ride... or maybe that's just your lover's parts down there talking, hmm? Maybe she wants to be scratched again?"

"What traitor?" Xander yelled, grabbing Spider by the arms and flipping her over, with his body nestled snugly between her legs. The effort made the tender flesh on his gut split, and the blood went right through Spider, and then he did too, slamming his nose against the concrete.

For a second, while they were translucent, their bodies were one. "I always wanted you inside me," she giggled, and it was Julie's giggle. "But, very well. You think you know who the traitor is. You said so only moments ago. But when I warned you of him, it was not a singular incident I was speaking of."

"You mean..." he gasped, trying to think of some other way to interpret what she was saying. "You mean that another friend is going to betray me?"

She smiled, but did not answer. "All good things come to those who wait, Womb. For right now, try and make it to the end of the month, hmm? Because what happens every month, will not happen this month. And you will lose everything, Womb. And then it will destroy you."

"Just show me what you mean!" he screamed, punching the floor and splitting his knuckles.

Behind him, the screen that had previously been blank flickered to life for one second, then dropped out again, the words 'waiting for signal' re-appearing on the screen.

Spider grimaced, then frowned. She turned and pointed, then faded away into the nothing again until only her voice remained. "It's everything you are, but it was made to hunt you down, Womb. Made to hunt us down. It is an Anti-Womb."

Xander looked toward where she was pointing. Another containment cell was there. This one was larger than the others, though... broader. As if someone with really thick shoulders were trying to fit inside. As he looked closer, he realized that this cell wasn't broken. The metal and glass on it were too wide for that. This one was just hanging open. Whatever had been inside it had escaped. He stepped closer and closed the lid, and the word engraved across its cover suddenly wasn't funny anymore.

It said Zakron.

CHAPTER SIX:
HUNT

Sunday, Day Five

Tommy pushed back the underbrush of the grounds as sweat poured off of him, slowly trickling down his back. His breathing was hard, and he wished that he had taken his mother's advice and brought a bottle of water along with him. He was deathly thirsty, and he could feel his blood sugar level drop with each passing second.

Right now, he couldn't care less. He could have dropped into a coma where he stood, and he still would have fought to keep moving. "Kerri!" he yelled at the top of his lungs, cupping his hands over his mouth. His voice was dry and crackling from the dehydration, so it didn't carry very far.

He stopped for a moment, holding his ear to the wind and praying for some kind of response. Anything that might let him think that he was on the right track, that he might be able to save the child, or help someone else save her. There was no response, only his echo and the sounds of other rescue workers calling out the same name.

Somewhere, Tommy realized, the girl's father was out there. And her friends. Her young friends at school would be wondering where she was. He wondered what their parents would tell them. How do you tell a child that their friend is gone, and that you'll try everything to get her back, but it might never happen? Or, worse yet, how do you tell someone that young that their friend is dead?

If you do it like Tommy's parents, you don't. You don't speak of it. And you make fun of him when you catch him crying in his room just a few weeks after seeing his friend murdered.

What do we tell our children? Do we give evil a name? Do we give it a face and a title, and show it to them so that they will run if they see it in the streets? No. They will have nightmares enough with their friends littering the ground.

No, we tell them that we will try harder. That we will protect them. That our love will keep them safe and warm. That nothing can hurt them.

And then when they are stolen in the night, Tommy scoffed, taking out a small piece of red tape and tying it around a tree. It was an approach that the rescue workers had begun to use to mark an area as searched. *Then we will cry ourselves to sleep and realize that we were lying to ourselves more than we were lying to them.*

Grunting to himself, Tommy pledged on into the night, trying to think more positively. He started working on the speech he'd give when he found and saved the girl.

Cathy sat in the padded chairs of the Turismo 3000

racing game at the Factory. She watched the animation as it played over and over again, a blank expression on her face. It was early morning, but classes had been unofficially cancelled. Most teachers were out helping with the search.

Her face was as white as a ghost, her eyes wobbly, unable to focus. The screen seemed blurry as the car on it turned this way and that to avoid other cars and road blocks, flipping over, then starting again looking like new. Her head started to tilt from side to side, following the car as it moved around the screen. She looked to be in some kind of trace, like she was caught in a cobra's eyes.

From across the room, Mike looked up from his shot at the seven ball, watching as she swayed back and forth.

"Again today?" Xander frowned, following his friend's gaze as he leaned against his pool cue.

Mike nodded, then turned back to his shot. He'd connected too far to the left and the cue missed the seven completely, scratching into the corner pocket instead. He sighed, slamming his fist lightly against the green matting.

Xander's eyebrows jumped as he waited for the cue ball to emerge from the hole on the side of the table. He took the ball in hand and placed it in the center of the table, firing at the seven and sinking it. He turned to shoot at the eight, then stopped, turning to Mike. "At the expense of my pool game, I'm gonna have to ask you what's on your mind."

Mike was still staring at Cathy from across the room, a girl who had slowly gone from white to green in the past few seconds. "She's been like that all day," Mike admitted, leaning against the table.

"Maybe she's upset. Didn't her sister used to babysit for Kerri? Maybe she knew the kid," he added, holding his gut as the true Womb churned.

Mike shook his head, "Naw. It's more than that. She's sick. She's sick and she won't let me help."

"What kind of sick?" Xander asked, joining Mike against the table, holding the cue stick against himself.

"When I picked her up at her house today, she was throwing up. Throwing up bad."

"What did you do?"

"Nothing. Couldn't. She was locked up in the bathroom. She tried to tell me she wasn't sick, but I could hear her gagging. Now look at her."

Xander frowned, turning back to the game and taking his shot at the eight. It connected, but the eight did not go in, it merely lingered by the hole. "This is so the worst time ever for this."

"Why's that?" Mike asked, turning to take his shot.

"Because of what's coming. Whatever this thing is, man, it took out the Womb and I don't think I hurt it."

"Things are taking you out all the time," Mike almost smiled, sinking the eight and lining up his shot at the nine.

"Yeah, but not the true Womb. This thing took out my worse half without a sweat. And then the dream with Spider... I know you don't buy into that, not sure I do, either... But she called it an Anti-Womb. Like maybe its equal and opposite force. Remember? From physics?"

Mike nodded curtly. "Whatever it is, it had better come soon. I don't know how much longer I can deal with this waiting." He took the shot, sinking the nine into the side pocket, then they both turned to watch Cathy again as she stared blankly at the cars driving across the game screen.

Tuesday, Day Seven

Xander landed against the thick branch of an evergreen tree, digging his claws into the bark to steady himself. The branch swayed a little beneath the added weight as he peered into the black of night that covered the forest. It was nearly eleven, and the chilled air was nipping at his skin like a tiny mutt with sharp teeth.

With a sound like ketchup being squirted out of a bottle, his eyes became cloudy and black, until they were a pure, reflective ebony. Suddenly, the forest was like day to him. He could see every nook and cranny of the trees, every bug on the leaves that were sparsely growing on low shrubs.

He breathed hard. He was about ten kilometers from the nearest house, and thirteen from where Kerri Walker had been abducted. He'd bolted here as fast as he could the second he heard his parents go to sleep, swinging from tree to tree to save time. Raising his nose into the air, he felt the womb-organ shudder and spurt as it diverted extra power into his sense of smell. He took a long sniff, then crouched on the branch like an acrobat, staring straight down at the ground.

He smelled fresh feces, dog hair mixed in it, telling him which species had made it. Nearby, another dog had sprayed its mark onto a shrub. But there was nothing ahead. This was the spot where the dog had stopped.

Carefully, Xander spun around the branch, letting go when his feet were parallel to the ground and landing safely, crouching beneath the foliage.

The dogs stopped here. This is where they got confused, Xander thought, scratching at the dirt a little and bringing some to his mouth, tasting it, then spitting it back out. *The police had given them Kerri's clothes, trying to get the hounds to find her. Here, the dogs kept running around in circles, not knowing where to go next.*

He bent down, putting his nose to the ground and sniffing hard, his eyes widening. *Her scent is strong here... but it keeps going, off to the west. Deeper into the woods. And there's something else...*

He popped all of the claws on both hands, crawling into the muck with his nose to the ground, licking out his tongue quickly every few seconds, just enough to taste the dirt. Suddenly, he stopped, sniffed twice, then pulled back dramatically. A deep growl formed in the back of his throat, as the Womb became excited.

Blood... he realized, and started slashing at the ground with his great talons, forcing the dirt out between his legs into a small pile, like a canine. About two feet down he stopped.

In the past few short months he had seen some of the most frightening, disturbing things that mankind had ever dreamed up, and he had faced them head on, but there in the woods, Xander Drew fell down on his hands and knees and began to cry. He cried in long, agonized howls, mucus streaming from his nose and mingling with the tears on the ground.

In the hole was the severed arm of a child, the scent of

which belonged to Kerri Walker.

Harry Ford's stomach lurched again, as even more vomit spewed from his lips out into the toilet bowl with a sickening splash. Tears ran from his eyes as the stomach acids burned his esophagus, giving them access into his blood stream. He grabbed a roll of toilet paper from a nearby roll and used it to wipe his lips, then tossed it into the bowl and flushed, regaining his composure.

He walked out to where his partner, Lance Berkshire, stood, staring down at the object in front of them.

Lance looked at his friend, placing a hand on his back. "You can go home, you know. I can do this on my own."

Harry shook his head, holding his hand to his mouth to keep from regurgitating again. "No. We have to find out everything we can. Besides, you shouldn't be alone."

Lance nodded, setting the timer on his tape recorder to zero and then pressing record. "Lance Berkshire and Harry Ford, Coral Beach Precinct Morgue. DNA results back, confirm identity of appendage as that of Kerri Walker, age seven."

Harry grimaced at the mention of the child's name.

"Arm was severed by what looks to have been sharp, jagged teeth from a side angle, slicing clean through muscles, tissue, and arteries. Possibly a member of the large canine or feline family. Definitely not human. Severing occurred just above elbow. Extreme bruising on back of arm and hand indicate a struggle at some point."

Harry stepped in, turning over the arm so that it was palm up. "More bruising on the palm, as well as cuts with some pebbles in them. Some nails missing, others with grit and grass beneath them, backing up the struggle theory. Blood capillaries ruptured beneath one nail," he stopped, moving his head so that he could see where the limb had been severed. "Clean cut, from sharp teeth. Foreign substance found within one of the bite marks... Lance, any word back from trace on what that was?"

"Yes," Lance stammered, now having to hold himself up against the cold, metal desk as he looked at the sheet of paper before him.

"Well, what is it?"

"Vaginal fluid. Her own," he gulped, laying down the paper.

"So the killer..."

"Yes."

"And then he..."

"Yes."

"Gawd..." Harry groaned, his eyes tearing up as he turned back toward the arm, looking at the skin around the bite. The flesh had turned black and blue, with some capillary action making crow's feet down the limb. He looked up, closing his eyes. "Oh, no."

"What?" Lance asked, rising to his feet.

"There's bruising around the bite."

Lance stopped, burying his face into his hands. "My god, Lance... she was alive when it did this to her. She might still be alive now."

Harry turned, bolting back to the bathroom to throw up again.

Thursday, Day Nine

Adam Genblade sat cross-legged facing a bare concrete wall, striped from the shadows made by the iron bars of his cell.

His bed was a springless mattress bolted to the floor. He was allowed absolutely no sheets and his mattress had no thread binding it together since he could use either to strangle a guard. His bathroom was a hole in the middle of the floor, and he was washed with a hose once a day. There was a sewage pipe running down one corner of his cell, protected by iron bars meshed so tightly that he could not get his hands into them. His meals were soft, mushy food usually consisting of mashed potatoes and turnip. His was permitted neither utensils, nor a plate, and was fed with a ten foot aluminum pole. Therefore, he had to eat, sleep, use the bathroom and take showers all on the same floor. Sanitation issues had been brought up many times since his incarceration, but they had always been overruled by the safety issues of the guards assigned to his care.

His auburn hair had become visibly darker since his imprisonment—it was no longer naturally lightened by the light of the sun—because his cell had only one small window which the sun never faced. His face had a cut across it: an accident with the aluminum pole while he was being fed the day before. His face was taut as beads of sweat formed on his head while he tried to concentrate, to relax himself despite his surroundings.

News of the little girl's disappearance had reached him today, along with the discovery of the child's arm. Silently, although he would never let anyone know, he prayed that the child would be alive. That Xander would find her safe and sound.

Suddenly, his eyes shot open, and he turned toward his barred window. His mouth dropped in shock, his pupils dilating in fear as he heard a slow scratch just outside it, which was overpowered by a maniacal growl. "Oh, fuck, no," Genblade cursed, unable to take his eyes off of the window.

Suddenly the scraping sound stopped, and there was a shuffling in the bushes, then it started again, fainter this time.

"...checking defenses..." Genblade mumbled, rubbing his temple as he tried to remember. "...locate structural weaknesses..."

He looked up, as the scratching again moved further down the wall, until now he could barely hear it. *Please, Xander,* he silently prayed, *figure it out soon.*

⋏⋎⋏

Chad walked down the dimly lit corridor, looking around frantically each time he turned a corner. About halfway down the long, tiled stretch, a knob protruded from the wall and he took off his duster and hung it there, unbuttoning the sleeves of his dress shirt. His jeans were tattered and worn, with dirt and grass stains all over them. He tracked it in, but the foot prints were barely visible in the low light.

Reaching the end of the hall, he pushed open the unlatched door that was waiting there for him, slowly rolling up his sleeve to reveal the red T that had been tattooed there.

Chad was a member of the Tees, a group of youth led by older men in Coral Beach and Glover Island that waged a minor war with the surrounding communities, with much major casualties. At the moment, they were in the middle of a feud between themselves and Coral Cove, the main headquarters of the Omega gang. A few weeks ago, many of their members had been injured by some kind of black demon calling itself a womb. A few days later, their newest member had shot a young man in the high school, making the cops search them out. They'd been forced to scatter. But now that the police had their hands full searching for the Walker child, which allowed the Tees to assemble again.

"Has she been found?" came a voice from the darkness, deep and scratchy.

"No," Chad frowned, his eyes glued to the floor. "But the police believe she's still alive."

"It does not matter anymore. We keep looking until the kidnapper is found and brought to justice. There is no need for acts *this* vile."

"Yes, master," Chad said, bowing a little.

Roulette stepped out of the shadows and lit a cigarette, the fire illuminating his face, painted white with a large T marked in red down the center. "See that whoever is responsible for this is found. We will conduct a proper search when our numbers are full."

"Yes, Roulette."

Saturday, Day Eleven
Mike pushed trees out of the way, wiping the sweat

from his brow as the warm sun beat down on him.

Xander, hanging from a nearby tree and using the height advantage to look around, flipped down next to his friend, sniffed the ground twice, then shook his head. "Nothing."

"Then we keep going," Mike said, cocking his head to one side and tying a marker onto a nearby shrub.

Xander nodded curtly in response, crouching down then leaping into the nearest tree, disappearing into its branches for a moment before jumping to the next. He poked his head out through the top of the branches, stuck out his tongue to taste the air, then crawled downward to speak to Mike again. "We head east," he said simply.

"East it is," Mike said, patting Xander on the back.

The pair started east until they reached a steep slope covered with rocks and unearthed trees.

Again, Xander landed next to Mike. "You can stop here if you want, bro. That might be hard for you to get back up."

Mike gave him a look.

Xander sighed, and they both started down the hill. "How's Cathy?" he grunted as a pointed rock drove into his knee, only to be forced out again by the healing factor.

"Wish I knew," Mike sighed honestly, gritting his teeth as he slid down the slope, the seat of his pants becoming dusty. "She hasn't talked to me since that day in the Factory. I went to her house, but her mother just gave me this look."

"What - ow - what look?"

"Like the ones Sara's mom used to give you."

Xander raised his eyebrows. "Oh. *That* look."

"Uh-huh," Mike said, as he propped himself up against a sideways-growing tree for support, taking a breather as he got ready to continue his trek down the hill. As he stared at the trunk, his eyes grew wide. "Xander!" he called out to his friend, who was a little further down the hill.

Xander turned, popping all of his claws and using them to help clamor his way back up the slope, until he sat alongside Mike. "What? What is it?" he gasped, fighting for breath.

"Just look," Mike said simply, motioning toward the tree.

There, carved into the tree, were three huge claw marks. Slowly, Xander took the claw he'd pulled from his face a week ago and placed it into the gouge. It fit perfectly.

"East," Mike said, his voice filled with more resolve than ever.

"East," Xander nodded, through gritted teeth.

ᙢ

Richard Ortega had abandoned his shirt twenty minutes ago, and now the red T tattoo was visible to the other four men that were trudging through the wilderness with them. They were so far out that their cell phones would not even work, yet they kept going. Everyone seemed to avoid the man with the tattoo, but not from fear. They left it alone because the man was helping.

Because it didn't matter anymore. Background, ethnic origin, money... even gang relation didn't seem to matter now.

All that mattered was finding the girl.

They'd become aware, one by one, that they were no longer even searching for the girl; they were searching for her body, but even that fact didn't seem to matter.

All that mattered was the girl.

The girl.

⋏⟨⋏

Monday, Day Thirteen

Officer Moony walked along the grass, leaves crunching underneath his feet. He stared out into the dimly lit woods nearby.

You were here, weren't you? he asked himself mentally, crouching down to a child's height. *No...* he remembered, scrunching over a few centimeters to the left, until he was at eye-level with a hole in the underbrush. *She saw you through the brush, pulled back the leaves, and then you took her, didn't you?*

Why? What was the big deal about her? What made her so special?

George Walker looked out his back window and watched as Moony bent down and prayed, his hands folded before him. Kerri's father stood, grim-faced, his frown twitching at the corners as he sipped on his steaming coffee.

He brought the phone back up to his ear, placing the coffee cup back onto his kitchen table. "Naw, naw. It's just the cop in charge a lookin' for Kerri, s'all. Now, lemme tell you somethin', I don't care what you've gotta do, just get them out there, all right? I want my little girl found, and I want her found now, you understand me?" he screamed, as he slammed the phone back down onto its receiver.

He chugged another gulp of his java down, the T on his shoulder standing out, like bright red soul-fire against the drab, white background of his kitchen.

His breaths were hard and labored, few and far between. He huddled in the corner of his cell late at night as the rain beat down outside.

All anyone could hear that night was the thunder and the rain, but Adam Genblade knew better. His ears picked up on more.

He could hear the unearthly shuffling just below his cell. The grunts and growls like only an animal could make. The sounds of talons and tendrils scraping against the moist concrete walls of his cell. The hisses. They were the worst. It only hissed when it was really mad. When it knew you were there. Like a snake right before it killed its prey.

"Look out!" Spider yelled, even as the Anti-Womb's massive talons ripped open Genblade's gut, exposing his organs for all to see in one massive spray of flesh and bile.

Genblade winced at the memory, lifting up his orange prison jumpsuit just enough to see the scar that the Zakron creature had left on him nearly four years ago.

Spider leapt to her lover's aid, tossing Genblade aside as she took out both of her swords, each one sparkling with ruby-encrusted arachnids. She smiled a little, blood oozing from the cut on her forehead down into her eye, making her blink.

It was all the thing needed. Tendrils spawned off of both its sides, going right through both of her wrists and lifting her up by them, making it impossible for her to get any leverage. The world's most elite acrobat, as incapacitated as a child.

Genblade tried to rise, but his intestines spilled out onto the ground. Everything went black and spotty, as the trees around him began to blend with the sky and ground.

Adam opened his eyes, sweat dripping down his brow as he recalled his encounter with the Anti-Womb. The beast had violated Spider in that battle and left her a quivering, broken mess for months. It had taken him three weeks to recover from the injuries he'd sustained. By the time he'd gotten out of the infirmary, Alpha had already captured Zakron again. It was back in its cell, where it would stay until they needed it.

It was our failsafe, he thought, remembering the word his former master had used. *It hunts and kills whatever it can, whatever's in sight. It was meant to be dropped on an area where a Womb had gotten out of control. Something that could stop it, stop anything...* he stopped, looking up at the window. For a second, he thought he saw two red eyes peering back at him, but there was a flash of lightning and they were gone. He shuddered. *I've got to get out of here. There's no way Drew'll be able to handle this on his own. That thing... it'll kill him. It'll kill everything. That little girl... she should consider herself lucky. They have no idea what this thing is capable of.*

Wednesday, Day Fifteen
Cathy walked down the hall of Coral Beach High school, hugging her books tightly against her chest as if

they were armor that would protect her. She felt dizzy and disoriented; her face as white as a ghost. The halls themselves seemed to fight with her, leaning in toward her in her skewed vision. The lockers wobbled and shone, the stickers and graffiti on them turning shapes and making demons. Her salvation was at the end of the tunnel.

Mike was just closing his locker door when he noticed her, and his smile was undeniable. There was no hiding his feelings for her, as he lay down his math book and walked toward her. "How are you today?" he asked softly, taking her gently by the shoulders and pulling her close to him.

Their bodies touched, and she pulled away. "I'm fine," she snapped, running a hand through her hair to make sure it was still okay. "Why?"

He was taken aback by her response. He'd asked her the same thing every day for as long as he could remember. "I dunno..." he stammered, shifting his backpack onto both shoulders. "I, uh, called your house last night and there was no answer..."

"Well, maybe I didn't want to talk to anyone, you ever think of that?" she huffed in frustration, grabbing her hair as if ready to pull it out before fiddling with the button on her tight jeans. "Do ever even think about anything, period?"

"Yeah, I think period is the operative word here," Mike grumbled, frowning.

"What?!" Cathy screamed, pushing Mike against his locker with as much force as she was able to muster, attracting the attention of surrounding students and teachers. "What did you just say?"

"I just... nothing!" he started, raising his hands in defense before turning to walk away. "I'll see ya later," he drawled, adjusting his backpack again.

Her eyes watered and her lower lip began to quiver as she watched him go until he turned the corner, then she collapsed in tears against his locker.

Reverend Robert Gallagher sat in the halls of The Apostle Church, his robes dancing along the stained hardwood floors. The pews were empty tonight, as they had been every night for weeks, and yet he had never seen the people of Coral Beach pray or look to the clouds for hope more.

It was ironic, he thought, that the first time everyone else in town turned to God at once was the only time that Gallagher himself had lost faith.

At the head of the church, rows upon rows of candles lay unlit, save for one. One candle burned brightly against the wind drifting in through the open windows of the cathedral, fighting against all odds to stay lit.

Walking toward it, he placed his hand over the flame, feeling its warmth for just a moment before licking his thumb and forefinger and snuffing it out with a sickening hiss. He crossed himself once, taking his collar from his neck and letting it fall to the ground, glad that nobody was around to see it.

"God, help me..." he whispered, as he prayed long into the night.

Friday, Day Seventeen

Black Womb touched down against the top of a high rock that almost peeked above the tree line, his chest heaving for air as his body melted into the shadows, becoming almost invisible to anyone who might think to look. In that moment he almost collapsed; he had to hold himself up against the stone beneath him. He had been searching for over one hundred hours straight, longer and harder than he'd ever pushed his powers, body, or mind before, searching for a scent, a shred of cloth, or anything that might even suggest that Kerri was still alive. That she still might be able to be rescued, if not saved. Even if they only found her for the sake of burying her, it was still that much more closure for her grieving parents.

But there had been nothing for days now, not a sight nor sound. Every few hours, someone would pass near him with a radio long enough for him to hear that the statistics of Kerri even being found dead were now less than ten percent.

There was also no sign of Zakron, the Anti-Womb. And yet, he was everywhere. As Xander's sleep-deprived mind began to rattle him, he saw the demon in every corner, under every stone. *I will find you,* he silently vowed to the killer, as he watched a lone man toting a shotgun patrol the trees below him, the low light of evening gleaming off the barrel. *I will find you because some things are unforgivable. Undeniable. Children should not have to be afraid to play in their yards, to go to school in peace, to walk down the street without fear of pain and murder. I will not stand for it. I am here, and I will keep being here, because this is not right.*

He turned, watching as a cadre of men both young and old stomped through the brush. He'd noticed them a few times, but never up close. They were quick and formidable, scouring the woods like a fine-toothed comb. There were thirty or so of them, some he recognized, some he didn't. But the symbol on their arms he recognized all too well.

They were Tees.

The Tees were searching the forests of Coral Beach, trying desperately to find the missing girl. *Because even those we thought were our enemies are here,* he realized, straightening up behind a tree to make sure he was not seen as he watched them pass, like silent military guerillas searching out their target, organized and elite, *because some things surpass rivalries and borders. Because the one and only thing all men have in common is a voice that screams in pain when it sees something as wrong as this. Tonight, we are not enemies. We are brothers.*

Randy Owchar looked up from his place at the back of the line of Tees, seeing the Black Womb as it stood perfectly straight upon its stone perch. Randy nodded once, and the Womb returned the sentiment of respect, as both men continued in their search.

⋏⟨⟩⋏

Cathy Kennessy sat with her mother on the cold, hard doctor's table. She wore only a small paper night gown, the kind with no back, and it made her very self-conscious to be so exposed. She tried to limit her time without her back to a wall, but right now she was sitting in the middle of the room.

"Okay," said the doctor cheerily as she snapped on

the second glove. "Let's see... Cathy, is it? Right, well, we might as well get started, shall we?"

When it was done the doctor frowned, then nodded at Cathy's mother.

⋏⋌

Sunday, Day Nineteen

"Let me out of here!" Genblade screamed in panic for the hundredth time, so much so that his throat was raw and bloody. "Don't you idiots realize what's happening?"

"Fire!" ordered Constable Lyle, as his men pumped Genblade full of tranquilizer darts, making the killer fade off to sleep.

"Idiots..." Genblade smiled, laughing slightly, before passing out on the concrete floor.

⋏⋌

Cathy sat on Xander's bed as he fiddled with the internals of his computer, sending sparks flying every few minutes as he tried to ground himself from frying his hard drive with static electricity. "Damn carpeted floors..." he mumbled, fumbling with his tiny screw driver.

Sweat was pouring down the girl's brow almost as much as the rain outside was beating against Xander's window. "Rain keeping you in?" she asked, almost absent-mindedly, not really caring about the response.

"The rain alone wouldn't, no," Xander grunted, kissing a burn on his finger. "But I tired the Womb out by forcing it to keep going for, oh, six or seven days. So, if I go out there right now, I'd probably freeze to death or die of hypothermia or something."

She nodded, although she had no clue what he had just said. She could hear little else outside of the rain pouring down. "What are you doing?" she sighed, as another spark flew toward her.

"Trying to get my sound card up and running, not that it'll ever actually happen. Fuck," he cursed, as an electrode snapped beneath his nail. "There goes another one," the Womb growled, stretching inside him, wanting to get out. It seemed the closer he got to Cathy, the more excited it became. He furrowed his brow, confused by the way it had been acting around her lately. He looked at her for the first time in over an hour. Her face had become white again, and she kept twitching and shuffling her hips, as if nervous or in pain. "Is something wrong with you?" he blurted, bluntly.

She turned to him, breaking her staring contest with the window. "Excuse me?!" she yelled angrily. "Rude much or what?"

"Sorry. I wouldn't have asked, but the Womb's acting up when I'm around you lately, and I just saw it as being kinda weird, is all."

She squinted at him, then tears began to fall down her cheeks. She collapsed onto Xander's pillow, and he immediately rushed to her side, trying his best to hold her. The Womb screamed. He ignored it.

"I'm sorry!" he exclaimed repeatedly, slapping himself upside the head. "There's nothing wrong with you! There's something wrong with me! I have someone living in my gut, seriously, can you believe anything I say?"

"Yes, there's something wrong with me..." she

screamed, her face already red from tears and anger.

"No, sweetheart..."

"There is! I'm stupid, and ugly and..."

"No, honey, you're not... you're adorable and loveable and..."

"Pregnant!" she yelled, burying her face into his arms, her tears drenching his shirt.

You never know when your life is going to change, he thought, as he held her close, unable to speak from pure, unadulterated shock.

Thursday, Day Twenty-One

Tommy and Xander pushed back a set of leaves, making the branches creak until they broke and splintered. The two of them had met up a quarter mile back and had worked together since, trudging through the damp, marshy woods after the rain. They had yet to speak to each other, as both men considered speech to be a waste of energy that could be better-spent searching.

"Stop," Xander said, putting an arm out in front of Tommy, who came to an abrupt halt.

"Who made you boss, Serial?" Tommy scoffed, slapping Xander's arm away.

"Shut up," Xander groaned, looking down solemnly.

"Why should I?"

Xander didn't respond, and it took Tommy a moment to notice him crying, his tears joining the rainwater on the ground.

Raising an eyebrow, Tommy solemnly pulled back the brush a few feet in front of Xander, even though he knew what he'd find there.

Laying in a puddle of reddish mud and leaves was the beaten, broken and naked body of Kerri Walker, her arm missing and her bowels ripped open, exposing her insides.

"Gawd..." Tommy choked, as he and Xander collapsed into one another's arms and cried. "... I really thought we'd save her..."

CHAPTER SEVEN:
THE END OF A GOLDEN AGE

Wednesday, Day Twenty-Two

The city wept.

Everywhere you looked, people were collapsing in the middle of the sidewalk as their grief overcame them. Some had not heard the news yet. When they were told, the wail that escaped from their lips was recognizable by all who heard it. It was the sound of innocence being lost, never to return. Stripped away, killed and raped in a dark forest.

Mike and Cathy held each other as they wept. Of everyone in the town, they had cause to -- more than anyone. It was not a good time to learn that he was going to bring life into this world, on a day when everyone was wondering if this earth was any place to raise a child.

Everyone was at school for a change. Xander, Julie, Tommy, Mike, Cathy... everyone. For once, there was nowhere better to go. There was no place where you could run to escape the pain, the sense that something beautiful had been stolen away from you. The knowledge that evil won out over good again. Not a word was spoken in the halls, only tears were shed and glances exchanged. Strangers patted each other on the back, trying their best to console each other and themselves, as Principal Snyder and Dr. Warren O'Toole patrolled the hallways, trying to help the student body in any way they could. No detention slips were given for punching lockers, fighting, or even graffiti. They all understood that these people were just taking it harder than others. That maybe they'd known the girl, or known someone who had.

Even the Tees cried. They stood in a circle, twenty men from all walks of life, bowing their heads in hours-long silent prayer for the soul of Kerri Walker. Their warehouse was again darkened, but candles erupted through the darkness now, as they fought to remain hopeful. Maybe, just maybe, they would get their shot at whoever committed this horrible act. Because vengeance is not just a word. It is a living, breathing thing that will not go unfed. It will–

Three straight lines were torn in the wall of the Tees' hideout, and they all gasped and shook as they turned to look. Daylight poured in, interrupted only by the movement of their attacker, just beyond their sight.

The wall was opened into a rough sphere, enough for it to step through, to the horror of all those within.

It hunched over on all fours. Completely black and shimmering, its inhumanly large muscles flexing erratically, its great chest inhaled and exhaled with massive bursts of oxygen, enough even that its breath could be mistaken for a strong gale by someone who did not know the difference. It had just three fingers on each hand, if they could be called that. They were more like jointed claws that sprung off of his palms, the inside track of which was even edged like a razor. Tentacles danced around its body in every direction, some even looked to be fighting with each other as they snapped about, like a lizard's tongue tasting the air for fresh scent. Its eyes were blood red and so dark that they were almost impossible to distinguish from its skin. The teeth were the worst, though. Protruding from where its lips should be, it had both a massive over-bite and under-bite, making the entire lower portion of its face nothing but row upon row of teeth.

It sniffed the air twice, then looked at all of them cowering and afraid to move. It began to growl.

"It's the Womb..." someone whispered in a hushed voice.

The creature sniffed again. There was a scent here that it had been following, the scent of another creature like itself. The other one had been here, weeks ago, but to its nostrils it was like yesterday. Its eyes darted from side to side, taking in every terror-filled face before it, and regarding each with as much dignity as a normal man would the food at an all-you-can-eat buffet.

Chad slowly pulled a gun from his leather duster, and a slow smirk slid over his dry, cracked lips. He wanted this. From the moment he'd heard about the body yesterday, he'd wanted this. The chance to kill something. Anything. To watch its blood bubble up to meet air and quietly trickle to the ground before coagulating and becoming hard, like a plug. He'd watched three people die in his life; the first was on his very first night as a Tee, when he was fifteen. But none of them would ever look or smell as good as this one.

Others knew better. Ian Char had faced the thing, which was now staring at them and sizing each one of the Tees up for dinner, before. He had lived to tell about it, to add to the hushed whispers in the alleys and side-streets, and contribute to the fearful tales of those who'd seen the darkness before. He touched the scar on the side of his face, still pink from over a month ago. The Womb had dragged him into the darkness, stopping him from killing a young girl, and ripped at his flesh to make him bleed. There hadn't even been time to scream or to see what was coming. There was only the sureness of death, and the sickening, hollow pain that came when he did not die. People who've had near-death experiences and claimed to be better for it were full of crap, Ian knew. In reality, you spend every day like a walking, talking corpse, waiting for death to find you. With a shaken gulp, Ian closed his eyes and waited, knowing that his wait was finally over.

The majority of them, however, felt the way Quinton Travers did, as he pulled out a long dagger, grasping it tightly in his hand and rubbing his thumb over the edge of the blade. Quinton felt vindicated, as if this thing had been brought here for a reason. The fear melted away as quickly as it came, and all that was left was the overwhelming need for vengeance. For themselves, for Kerri, for everything. He smiled devilishly, locking eyes with the beast and licking his lips. "Come on, boys," he said, his southern accent abundant. "We got us some killin' to do."

As if on cue, the beast attacked them, leaping with all the power contained within its hind legs, as if catapulted into the sky by some invisible force. They all watched as the thing silently flew through the air, their heads circling to see where it would land, like an audience watching a man being shot from a cannon at the circus. It landed in the center of the circle they had formed, and for the briefest of moments, some of them rejoiced, thinking that they had it surrounded.

With inhuman speed it lashed out, jumping again the second it hit the ground. It leapt straight up, grabbing onto either side of one man's hips and digging his claws in deep, breaking three ribs and puncturing the liver, both kidneys, and the appendix. Blood started to fill all four organs immediately, and soon it would be spilling over into others and onto the floor. The man screamed as the others around him backed away and nearly jumped out of their skins. The monster roared, and as it did, slobber escaped from its mouth and splashed onto its victim's face.

Behind the demon, Travers snarled. "Shoot him, you morons!" he yelled, waving at Chad and the others.

Three of them pulled out handguns and started to fire, emptying round after round into the thing's back. It did not flinch, even as chunks of its flesh spray-painted the wall behind it a sickly black. It ignored the bullets as if they were not even there. Instead, it opened its mouth wide. For a moment, nothing seemed to happen. More Tees fired, but still nothing happened, and the sound of gunfire made everyone's ears ring, so it was like there wasn't even any sound. It was like watching a silent movie, and that made it even scarier. There was no sound to evoke emotion, to tell you how to feel about what you saw. Only the raw, true sickness of life. With that, the demon's jaw bone popped out of place with two hard snaps, like a baseball bat connecting with a ball for the first time, and buckling a little under the strain. A small amount of black liquid mixed with its drool as its broken jaw lowered, expanding as it went, like an elastic with a weight on one end. Within moments, it was half the length of an average man's body. The demon lunged forward, as its victim silently screamed, forcing half of the victim's body into its mouth. It raised its head, and like a humanoid anaconda, let the body slide down its throat. It stopped just below the pelvis, biting hard and letting each leg topple uselessly to the ground. Its jaw returned to its normal size, shrinking back like the monster was winding it in from behind. Then it licked its lips with a long, slobbering, forked tongue, and turned to face the rest of them.

As one, the remaining Tees turned to run for the back exit. Anyone who had glanced back in time to see would swear that they saw the creature smile.

It let out another massive leap, landing on the back of one man and driving him into the ground, his face smashing against the concrete as the monster's toe-claws burrowed into the back of his skull, then retracted, leaving brain matter on the bottom of its foot. It reached out to one side and grabbed another, pulling him close and biting off his head before the boy could even manage a scream. Blood squirted upward as his heart continued to pump in the still-twitching body. Tentacles lashed out, whipping at another two Tees' feet, cutting off all four feet with the sharpened ends and leaving them to scream and try to crawl for the exit, not realizing that they would bleed out long before they reached it.

The rest of them got out the back way, slamming the door shut behind them as if that would slow it down. Calmly, it sliced through the door and stepped out through. One man had tripped and fallen and was trying to clamber his way back up when he turned and saw the beast looming over him. He closed his eyes and waited for it. It lingered for a moment, then bent down. Suddenly, it stopped. It sniffed the air twice, then turned its head to the east.

Off in the distance, almost beyond sight, was Coral Beach High School.

It pivoted on a dime and started sprinting in a bee-line straight for it on all fours, kicking up dirt as it bolted across the road, disappearing between two buildings, leaving the fallen Tee to scramble to his feet and take off in a mad dash for safety.

"Xander?" she called out, her voice tiny and weak.

He smiled at the mere sound of it, though he did not understand why. He turned to see Julie, her hands clasped together at her pelvis, head down, looking like a child waiting to be scolded. And yet, she had a smile on her face, as she always did, somehow. She was wearing a plaid shirt and matching skirt, with high stockings and white gloves. Dressing as a Catholic school girl was probably the most polar-opposite thing she could have worn considering her personality and yet he found it looked good on her. Amazing, actually. He scratched his head, trying to recall the last time he'd noticed what a girl was wearing and had actually cared. "Hey, Julie. How are you?"

She bit her lip, tilting her head to one side, then the other, as if weighing out her life to decide how to respond. "Pretty good, all things considered," she said, finally. "I'm kinda freaked, though. I mean, I know this sounds awful, but it's not even the fact that all these things happened to this poor girl, y'know?"

Xander nodded, reached out and stroking the side of her arm. "I know. It's not awful."

"All I can think about is, like, what if that had been Mandy or Cathy or someone?" she continued, as they both moved over to the wall and sat against it.

"Or you?" he furthered, smiling at her.

"Is that selfish?" she admitted, gritting her teeth for what she expected would be a mean, and therefore truthful, response.

"Not at all. In fact, that was pretty much all I could think of at the time too."

"Worried about Cathy? She is going through a lot."

"No," he frowned, shaking his head. "I was more worried about you."

She looked at him, her face unsure of whether to be happy or puzzled, but settling on both.

"Even when I found that body, I couldn't help but think of everything that's been done to you. Phillips, Derek, everything. I guess... I guess when I was out there, looking, I had time to think about all that. Time I didn't have before. And I guess I realized how much of a big deal it is that you trust anyone, let alone me," he looked down, clenching his fists. "You wanna talk selfish? I didn't even care about that girl, or whether I found her alive or not. It was more about saving you, or Cathy, or..."

"Sara," she nodded, taking his hand and making it relax instantly.

"Yeah. And now I gotta wonder if that's why she died. I already blame myself so much, now I have to deal with the fact that maybe, subconsciously, because I didn't care enough, because my mind wasn't in the game, I didn't stop this on purpose. Maybe I should've been out looking for her killer, maybe I should have just stayed home and helped you and Cathy..."

"Shh," she soothed, wrapping her arms around his head and pulling it to her chest, stroking the back of his neck. "I'm safe. Cathy's safe. It's all gonna be okay."

Suddenly, Xander's body lunged, shaking in Julie's arms. The true womb fired up, screaming one undeniable instinct into his brain and burning it there in letters ten feet high: hide. Not fight, not run...just hide. The urge was so great that it took all his strength of will just to keep himself from transforming right there in her arms. "No," he gulped, swallowing back blood, bile, and blackness that was rising in his throat. "Nothing's ever going to be okay again."

ʎϪ

Cathy and Mike were both still crying, holding each other in their arms. Everyone that passed them was ignoring them. They knew that their grief was different, that there was more, but there was no use to trying to help. "How could this have happened?" Mike choked, swallowing hard. "I mean, we used protection... didn't we?... We used a condom..."

She frowned, nodding, the tears shaking from her

chin. "They're not one hundred percent, remember? What Miss Hall used to say? Only abstinence is one hundred percent."

"Don't lecture me," he snapped, biting his lip.

"I didn't... at least, I didn't mean to," she pleaded, her face turning the same red as her cheeks.

"I don't need this. I don't. And how long have you known?"

"Days. Mom knew first, though. I just didn't know how to tell you. I was even going to try and get Xander to do it."

"Xander knew!?" he yelled, clenching a fist , then letting it go as fast as it had. He stopped, calming himself, then looked her squarely in the eye, his voice almost malicious. "Am I the father?"

"What?" she squealed, her voice barely human through her tears.

"Am I the father?"

"How can you even ask me that? Who else would it be?"

"Oh, I dunno," he shrugged sarcastically, rolling his eyes at her, demeaning her. "He's short, stupid, a superhero, and his last name is the past tense of 'draw.' Who do you think? He's got all these powers, maybe one of them is super-sperm?" he curled his lip, giving her a look of pure disgust. "Or maybe you didn't even make him wear one, hmm? Can't get enough of that dark and mysterious skin, right?"

"You are the only person I've ever been with!" she pleaded, grabbing him by the pant leg and practically begging at his feet now. "You're the only person I ever loved!"

"Is this how you treated Grendel?" Mike yelled, not even turning to face her as he stormed off toward the stairs in rage, "because if you did, let's give the poor guy the good boyfriend of the year medal."

"Michael!" she screamed, getting up and running after him frantically.

Suddenly, the wall beside her was gone.

There was no warning, no screams, no sounds of cracking plaster for five minutes beforehand like in the movies, just the crash and the sudden feeling of debris smashing against her head and body, forcing her to the ground, then the sounds of screams as everyone ran.

Mike turned, sweat already pouring down his face. He could see nothing at first, then the dust began to settle. At first, all he saw was Cathy, the love of his life, barely breathing under a cover of plaster and concrete.

Then he saw what stood over her.

It took a step forward, and the ground shook, cracks forming in the floor. Its teeth were disproportionately massive, even compared to its huge body, with muscles that normal anatomy books hadn't even discovered yet. The claws on its feet tapped against the ground it stood on, like a normal person tapping his fingers as he decided what to order at a restaurant. It sniffed the air twice, despite the fact that it had no nose. All in all, the thing looked like Black Womb on steroids, a notion that made Mike shiver in fear. "Zakron," he whispered, and the name wasn't funny. It was terrifying. Looking up at this monster, Mike suddenly felt a great swell of pity for any criminal that ever had to look up and see Xander come at them.

The creature turned toward Mike suddenly, like a dog whose name had just been called. It leapt, pushing both hands and feet against Mike's body and forcing him against a locker. The metal door bent in and broke, leaving the shards to dig into the boy's back, drawing blood immediately.

"Argh!" he screamed.

As soon as he did, Cathy moved, as if his cry had given her new life. She slowly pushed the debris off her back and stood, stumbling a little as she limped toward the beast. "Leave him alone!" she ordered, but her voice shook almost as violently as her body as she struggled to hold her own arm in place.

Zakron looked at her for a moment, its eyes dancing over her. Again it sniffed twice, then grunted, stepping back a pace, almost as though it was afraid. For a split second, Cathy thought that maybe simply standing her ground would scare it off, like a dog with more bark than bite.

Then it lashed out, slapping her across the mid-section with one violent blow, sending her sailing through the air. She landed on her side in the middle of the stairwell, her body cracking loudly and going limp. She bounced once, like a ball, then rolled the rest of the way to the bottom of the stairs, hitting the far wall and not moving again.

"Murderer!" Mike yelled from behind the killer.

It turned just in time for Mike's fist to connect with its face.

Again, the creature did not even flinch.

Mike pulled back to punch again, his face livid with

anger.

This time, Zakron caught the fist in mid air. The beast twisted it sharply, forcing Mike's elbow to pop out of place, then held him up by it, exposing the boy's side. One swift motion with his other hand opened him up, spilling blood onto the floor.

It sniffed the air again, turning to the south and growling, then leapt out the hole it had created in the wall.

Mike lay there a long moment, not knowing whether he should try to move or not. Cathy was dead, he was sure of it. He'd seen a lot of people hurt and killed in his short life, and by this time he knew what a person looked like when they were just unconscious and when they were dead. The subtle differences in how they fell and rolled, the way their eyes looked. Even the color of their skin changes. It alters in tint just a little. Blood gushed out of his mouth and his side, his wounds stinging from the urine that was escaping him, as he lay there and wished for death.

"Mike!" Xander yelled, and it sounded like he was underwater. "Mike, what happened!?" he demanded, kneeling next to his friend and turning him over, only then noticing the slice going up his side. "Oh my god."

"Dead..." Mike mumbled, blood gurgling out of his throat until he feared he might choke on it. He prayed that coppery tang would not be the last sensation he experience before death.

"You're not dead, Mike," Xander frowned, snapping his fingers before his friend's eyes. "Now, tell me what happened here!"

"Cathy's dead..."

Xander's eyes grew wide as he looked past Mike, and saw Cathy's limp body crumpled at the bottom of the stairs, not breathing. Not moving. He turned toward the gaping hole in the wall just inside to see Zakron disappear into the woods that led to the penitentiary. "Oh no you don't," he snarled as he pulled out a knife and sliced open his own wrist, letting darkness seep out and work its way over his entire body.

"Black Womb lives."

CHAPTER EIGHT: ANTI-WOMB

"No, no, no, no..." Genblade repeated over and over again, as he paced back and forth in his cell, scratching at the rash that had formed around the flesh where the tranquilizer darts had dug into him. "This is how it starts. You take one. When they find it, they'll grieve. They'll go to old habits. He's watched them. He knows what they'll do, where they'll go, where they'll be, that's how he'll take them out. Womb doesn't know. Why hasn't he come? Why not ask for help? Moron. Moron! Doesn't he understand what this is? What it'll do to him and everyone else around him? He should kill them all now and save them the pain. Hell, even I'd do that much," he wiped the sweat from his brow, then looked up at his window suddenly, then turned back toward the hall. "You're here, aren't you?"

Adam Genblade stayed silent then, positioning his feet and hands into a fighting stance, determined not to go down without a fight.

He heard it then, far away. It seemed like miles off,

like some battle being fought on the distant horizon that was no worry to him. He heard the gunshots and the pounding of the steel doors followed by the slow creak as they buckled. He heard screams. Horrible, blood-curdling screams, the kind that he used to inflict on a daily basis. He recognized the tactics... the forwardness of it. There was no emotion to it, no stopping to gloat or even speak. It was efficiency, nothing more, nothing less. The Anti-Womb was a far more effective killing machine than he, Spider, or even Black Womb. Or all of them combined, really.

A guard squashed up against the bars of his cell, sending spurts of red liquid from his mouth and ears before bouncing to the floor. He'd been thrown; he was dead before he even hit the bars. Genblade didn't move, did not so much as twitch even as Zakron stepped forward, breathing heavily from the lust of the kill.

"Always knew I'd go down in a good brawl," Genblade laughed, smiling a little with his toothy grin.

൜

Black Womb rounded the curb, the penitentiary finally coming into sight. His black, scaled muscles tensed and relaxed with every step, shimmering brightly in the morning sun. His eyes were bright and red, darting from side to side at all times, marking everything around him and instinctively taking note of it. His claws were out, ready to strike at any moment. He was about to transform into the Xander Drew guise when he saw the two front doors ripped apart and realized how unnecessary it was. Before he even reached the entrance of shredded metal, he knew every guard inside was dead.

He stepped inside and the stench was overwhelming: the smell of bowels and bladders spilling their contents in the seconds after death. There were ten of them in the main hall alone, some were missing arms, others missing heads. It looked like something out of a Stephen King novel, the way they were arranged like the way a hamster arranges the things in its cage. The entire floor was a puddle of blood and urine that was almost a centimeter deep, but it may as well have been ten feet high, because within his second skin, Xander felt like he was bathing in it. *All this time... almost a month now, I could have stopped this... and didn't. And look who's paying the price. Cathy, Mike, and all these cops... this ends here, my idiot little cousin. You think you can stop me by growling and flashing your claws? You're up against the Reality TV generation, man. Time to play rough.*

He turned the corner to go down the hall toward the holding cells and almost smiled. Genblade's cell was wide open, ripped off of its hinges. *I'd like to see you beat me and Adam, freak. You're in for it now.*

Black Womb entered Genblade's cell just in time to see Zakron rip the copper pipe from the wall of the room, and swing it so fast that neither man could see it, let alone react to it. As water spilled everywhere, drenching all three of them, the pipe dug into Genblade's gut, forcing its way in. Immediately, blood started pouring out of him, the pipe keeping the wound perfectly round and open. It was like seeing blood put on tap. A normal person would be dead within seconds. He gave Genblade ten minutes, at most.

Genblade turned toward Xander, mouthing something indiscernible, then hit the floor with a splash.

The water came down like rain, like tiny explosions upon them both. For a moment, they just stood there. Each of them looked at the other, like seeing a fun house reflection of themselves. Polar opposite, yet with so much in common. So different that they were the same.

Suddenly, Xander felt a pang in his gut. He looked down to see that Zakron's hand was inside of him. He could feel the monster's claws wrapping around his intestines, swirling them around its claws before yanking hard, pulling them into view. "Arrh!" the Womb yelled, his entire body spraying in all directions. He hadn't even seen the blow coming, hadn't noticed the lunge. Nothing was that fast. It wasn't possible.

He felt an impact against his head, and opened his eyes in time to see the concrete wall coming at him. Again, he felt the trauma as his brain rattled back and forth inside his skull, and everything was black except for a few stars that shone brightly in the corners of his eyes. He felt something snap inside his mouth, and he swallowed one of his massive, sharp teeth. Deep inside him, he felt the womb push hard, then again... then finally give up, relaxing. As the black ooze started to melt off of him, and the face of Xander Drew started to become visible, he turned to look at Genblade, who was as good as dead on the floor. Then he looked at Zakron, standing there and waiting for its prey to fall while it remained untouched. *We didn't even get one blow in.* He almost laughed, defeated, as his knees gave out and he hit the ground, his eyes rolling back into his head.

Xander swallowed hard, a large glob of blood traveling down his throat.

He had to swallow at least once every few seconds, or the red fluid spraying from the artery in the roof of his mouth would start to flow out past his lips. His eyes were foggy and he tried desperately to hold his guts inside of him, his throbbing intestine threatening to spill out onto the floor.

Blackness was melting off of him, dripping onto the dull concrete floor. Blood flowed by his feet, hurrying to a drain in the center of the room.

His head weaving back and forth from exhaustion and dizziness, he managed to hazard a glance toward the officers that lay around him. Some were missing limbs. The rest were missing heads. He felt their blood wash past his feet, and as he did, his eyes went to another victim.

As he felt himself slipping away, he looked up at the hulking mass of flesh which had done all of this, and his eyes filled with a new terror at the renewed sight of the squirming form of black flesh and teeth and claws.

Uttering one last attempt at breath, Xander fell, his body crashing to the floor and his eyes rolling back into his head. His last thought was wondering how he'd let this sneak up on him. How he'd let his entire world come crashing down around his ears, when he'd had so long to stop it...

No!

No!

"No!" he screamed, pushing against the cold, wet floor with both hands, flipping himself upward as he willed the ooze to wrap back around his skull. He jumped back to his feet, twirling once and kicking Zakron square in the mid-section, sending the beast back a step. It grunted, staring at him as if he'd done something wrong. "I do not go out like this!" he screamed, lashing out with his claws and raking them against his enemy's face. To his relief, he drew blood. But it was gone in a moment, as the wounds healed over even faster than he had made them, the blood soaking into the creature's flesh and reintegrating itself into its form.

I drew blood, Xander thought, wanting to throw a parade for himself on that fact alone. *You can be hurt, which means you can be killed. All I need is the time to figure out how.*

He flipped backward, kicking Zakron in the chin with both feet. He landed on his hands and then flipped again, until he was out in the hall. "Hey, Zach!" he yelled tauntingly, cupping his hands over his mouth for effect. "Your mother was Molly!"

The Anti-Womb's brow slanted. It did not comprehend the words, but their meaning was all too clear. Even an animal knows when it's being mocked. It took a step forward, then another, quicker, and leapt at Xander with its teeth and claws outstretched.

Quickly, Xander pulled the broken door to Genblade's cell in front of him. Zakron slammed against it, breaking off three of its teeth. It snarled as it tried to force its way through, its slobbering tongue seeping through the bars, trying to get at him. Just to get a taste.

There was a groan of metal, and the Womb's red eyes became wide with fear until they were almost spherical. The iron bars were giving way under the power of Zakron's great jaws. Its teeth were cutting through the metal.

Plan B! Xander thought promptly, forcing his feet

against the cage and pushing back with all his strength, sending both Zakron and the cell door flying backward into the wall.

"Zaaa-Kroan!" the creature bellowed, so loud that the walls seemed to shake. It batted the door away as if it were a fly, getting to its feet and looking around to see if it could find Xander. It turned left, then right, but the boy was nowhere in sight. It growled and shuffled, sniffing at the air. The water still pouring down from the broken pipe made it impossible for it to get a good lead on the scent of its prey. It turned its head up and barked twice, its Adam's apple bobbing rhythmically as it tried to use its incredible ears like a bat's sonar.

Again, nothing.

It grunted, bending down until it was almost on all fours again, scratching at the ground with its massive claws.

"Hey, numb-nuts," came a scratchy, deep-throated voice from behind. It turned, and as soon as it did, it felt an enormous pressure on its mouth and throat, followed by the taste of metal and another taste it did not recognize. The Womb smiled, savoring the moment before turning the valve to the fire hose.

Immediately, hundreds of tons of water pressure forced its way down Zakron's throat, forcing him back against the far wall.

It won't kill him, Xander had to remind himself, to keep him from getting too ahead of himself. *I can survive without breathing through my nose and mouth, it's a safe bet he can too. But it might slow him down for a-*

Zakron reached up with one blurred motion, cutting

the fire hose just below the valve, then swallowed the nozzle and whatever else was in his mouth at the time, letting out a loud burp. Urine trickled down its leg and it got up, shaking, spraying everything around it with water, like a wet canine.

Plan C... Xander thought, as the creature charged at him again, as silent as ever. He ducked, diving out of his adversary's path, and rolling along the ground, coming up on his feet and breaking into an immediate run. *Gawd, what I wouldn't give for a plan 'C' right about now.* He turned to look over his shoulder, only to see Zakron right behind him, and gaining fast. *Can't stay in here... he's too big. He's got too much room on me in such an enclosed area. I've gotta get him outside.*

He turned the corner on his heel, Zakron nipping at his ankles as he leapt for the exit, rolling against the dirt and gravel outside, smudging it against his shimmering hide. People turned, awestruck, unable to move as the two monsters squared off, turning to look at each other like gunslingers in some old western. *This is it. This isn't an enemy that can be reasoned with. Only one of us is coming out of this alive... but so help me, if I go down, you'll choke on me and die yourself, you sadistic bastard. No way are you living, not after what you did to that girl...*

Zakron leapt high, but this time Xander made no effort to dodge the attack. Instead, as the public watched in horror, he leapt as well, and the two equal and opposite forces met head on.

Paramedics arrived at Coral Beach High school as students huddled together, trying to make sure their friends were okay. Nobody paid much attention as Julie and Mike cried, looming over but afraid to touch the broken, beaten body of Catherine Kennessy.

"Get out of the way!" one paramedic screamed, waving for both of them to move. Julie jumped up right away, but Mike stayed there, still as a marble statue and looking down at the woman he loved as blood poured from his body, but he paid it no mind. It was of no consequence to him.

He was pushed out of the way and backed up a few steps silently, as two men laid a stretcher out between him and his love. They hoisted her up onto it, and immediately the clean, white sheet turned to dark red. Blood seeped out from between her legs, and she did not move. Never once did she move. He reached out and touched her hand, and it was chilled, her lips blue.

Soft

Lime

Tender

Moist

Wet

stop.

"She's so cold," he said in a hollow voice, as he watched them wheel her away into the back of an ambulance. Julie slowly walked up behind him, reaching out and grasping his hand, then wrapping both arms around him, bawling into his shirt. He turned to her, surprised that she was there, having not noticed her before. He stroked the back of her head, his stare falling past her to the rubble at their feet. "Should we get her a blanket?"

CHAPTER NINE:
ZAKRON

Black Womb hit the pavement, which buckled up and folded beneath his weight. Blood shot out of his mouth through the artery that had ripped itself open moments ago, splashing against a nearby car windshield. His head knocked back, and he felt the blinding pain of his neck breaking, then immediately healing itself again. It was like feeling it break twice, and as splotches of light dotted his vision and he lost control of his limbs, he momentarily cursed his healing factor for letting him live. Glass protruded from his right eye as his healing factor slowly worked it out. Strangely, he could still see out of that eye, but it was like looking through a prism. It looked like there were ten enemies, ten Zakrons. For a moment, the notion petrified him. *Nothing's ever hit me that hard,* he realized as he tried to move, but found that his body didn't want to obey him yet. His leg twitched once, and that was the most he got. *Not Genblade, not Blackheart... nothing. Not even the explosion that leveled the Engen building hit me that hard.* "Hey, ass-wipe..." he coughed, gurgling blood, "Is that the best you... got? |..."

And for the first time since my mother made the mistake of teaching me to talk, I'm speechless. It's just standing there, waiting for me to attack. Waiting for me to strike again, so it can knock me on my ass again. It's not even trying to kill me, it's just batting me around, like a cat with a mouse.

So what do I do when some big bastard sits there and waits for me to hit him?

Oblige.

The Womb pushed off of the ground, leaping to his feet again, then crouching down until his body was like a coiled spring, letting go and zipping through the air like a bullet with his claws extended. He connected with Zakron's face, sending both creatures sprawling backward into a roll. Xander dug his talons deep into his enemy's skull, pulling as hard as he could, trying to rip the behemoth's face off. They rolled more, and Xander shut his eyes, screaming with effort as he tried to tear off a chunk of flesh. When he opened them, Zakron was on top of him, smirking.

Oh... fuck.

It raised a giant arm, slamming it down on Xander's skull, driving it into the ground.

-SLAM!-

-SLAM!-

-SLAM!-

Again and again, it beat on him, forcing its weight upon him, until it grabbed him around the neck and slung him to one side. His body smashed through the windshield of a car and landed in the front seat, bouncing against the comfortable leather. "No, that's all right everyone. No need to thank me," he groaned in a small, whiney voice. "What's that Jenna Jameson? You have a twin sister? Well, if you think she'd like to join, I won't object..."

He tilted his head up, looking around. Slowly, a wry grin spread over his lips as he saw the keys dangling in the ignition, jingling against the steering wheel. *About time I got a little luck,* he thought, sitting up in the driver's side of the Beetle and revving the engine, shifting gears into drive. *I've thrown everything I've got, and you've kept coming. Now, I'll throw everything I can find.*

Slamming his foot to the accelerator, the car sputtered to life and started forward, bouncing over detritus material and wasted lamp posts, aiming straight for Zakron. "Now, you son of a bitch!" the Womb yelled, slapping the steering wheel. "Reap the whirlwind!"

Zakron reached up, coming down upon the car with a giant claw, slicing into the hood and right down through the frame. The car continued forward under its momentum, being sliced right down the middle like a tin can, splitting on either side so that neither half even touched its intended target. When the dust cleared, Zakron was standing exactly where he had been, except now he was holding Black Womb by the neck, slowly squeezing it, forcing pressure into his skull until eventually his head would pop like a grape. It growled, and the sound was almost like the purr of a cat. As Xander choked on his own blood, he realized that this thing was happy.

Xander grunted, shifting within the creature's massive grip, pulling at its fingers with his claws, swinging back and kicking it in the chest. "Hey, precious," he whistled, fighting for the creature's very limited attention. "Wanna see a trick?" He opened his mouth wide, biting down on Zakron's thumb with all the power in his jaw, snapping it off. The creature howled, loosening its grip until Xander fell to the ground, spitting out the appendage. "Yeah!" he screamed triumphantly, turning and walking a few steps away to where a broken street light lay. "You like that, huh? Is that the way it felt for her, I wonder? Are you even feeling a fraction of the fear that she felt, you half-wit? Lemme tell you somethin'," he chuckled, straining a little as he picked up the long, metal pole. "Your pain is just beginning. I'm gonna give you everything you've dealt out in spades, baby!" He turned with a sick grin, holding up the lamp like a baseball bat, ready to connect it with Zakron's head.

Zakron's claw connected with his gut, sinking deep inside, squirming around inside of him again, jiggling at his internals. He dropped the lamp-post to the ground with a sharp clang, the agony steaming out of every pore on his face, his every muscle becoming as tense and strained as stone.

"If you can't fight fair..." the Womb gagged, blood running from his lips. Quickly, he reached down, his claws digging into the demon's groin and pulling up, slicing straight to its chest.

"Argbda!" it yelled, tossing Xander again and smashing him into the side of the glass office building behind them.

"I'll bet you say that to all the girls, you handsome devil, you," Xander hacked, glass falling out of his body as he again picked up the lamp post. Swinging it high above his head, he brought it down across Zakron's back, knocking it to the ground with a thump. *He hit the ground!* Xander screamed inside his own head, as he drew back and hit the creature again, this time across the face, shattering the lamp bulb into its cheek and sending it onto its back. In his head, audiences were applauding him, like a runner sliding into home base at the bottom of the ninth. He drew back again, his smirk a mile long. Suddenly, tentacles grew out of its back, eight of them stretching up and catching the pole in mid-air. "Oh, come on..."

It lifted the pole high, taking Xander with it on the opposite end, then slammed it into the glass wall of the office building, sending millions of shards of broken glass deep into Xander's body, puncturing a lung and his heart all at once. Glass hit the ground with the slow, steady twinkling of raindrops, followed by the slump of Xander's beaten body.

Moaning, he forced himself to his feet, turning slowly to see Zakron calmly walking toward him, untouched. Unharmed. *Fuck this,* Xander thought as the Womb burned the word 'hide' into his skull again. Only this time, he listened. He scrambled to his feet and started to run for home, the glass digging further and further into his feet with every step, but he didn't care. *I've got to get away. This is insanity. I'm no good to anyone dead, and it's not going to bring Cathy or Mike or Genblade back to life if I get myself killed. There's got to be a better way than this. It's like this thing knows me, knows my every move, my every instinct...*

From behind him, Xander heard a woman's scream. He turned to see Zakron, standing right where he'd left him, holding up a girl no more than fifteen. It smiled wickedly with that big, toothy grin of his. *And so help me, it knows exactly what to do to reel me back in.*

"Hey!" the Womb yelled, jumping onto the hood of a car and using its momentum to force him onto the side of a nearby building, ricocheting off of it toward the ground, until he was again within ten feet of the Anti-Womb, looking straight into the eyes of death. "Our first date isn't even over, and already you're cheating. I knew mother was right about you..."

Zakron grunted passively, throwing the girl into the air.

"No!" Xander yelled, as the girl flew toward the sharp, metal wreckage of the Beetle he'd tried to drive. He leapt forward, diving out with both arms, retracting his claws as fast as he could, closing his eyes in fear. He felt an impact on both forearms, and opened his eyes long enough to see the girl in his arms before he slammed back-first into the wreck.

"Thank you..." the girl stammered, recoiling in fear of her savior.

"Just get out of here!" he yelled at her, sprouting his claws again. He turned, watching as Zakron slowly walked toward him with a macho strut, almost gloating. Xander laughed as he felt something trickle by his feet, an odd smell filling the air and making him want to vomit even more than he already did. *I wish he'd talk,* Xander thought, squinting and sizing up his enemy as the distance between them lessened, *I wish he'd gloat or call me names or something. The silence is deafening.* "This is where you get off," he said simply, striking his claw against what was left of the car's metal frame, creating a spark that traveled slowly to the pavement, igniting the gasoline that was pooled in a small pot-hole there.

ᐱᐸᐳ

Black Womb's head was lodged against the remains of a street sign, his body broken and sprawled in several different directions, like a bent compass. He opened his eyes, and the light burned him almost as bad as the flame that had churned up around him, igniting his flesh. The blackness was melting off of him, and no amount of will power was going to bring it back now. After a beating like that, he wondered if it would ever come back again. "I got you," he breathed harshly, his throat raw from inhaling smoke and fire. "I got you..."

He chuckled, slowly sitting up to look around. There was fire everywhere. After he'd lit the gas, there had been at least two more explosions from nearby cars, slinging his body in one direction after another. But the pain would heal. His bones would knit. All that mattered now, was that he'd-

"No," he whispered in shock, as a form stepped through the smoke in front of him, walking over the flame as if it were nothing. Again, Zakron was looking down at him, unscathed. "It's not possible."

"Zaaa-Kroan!" it bellowed, opening its monolithic jowls.

"Right, then," Xander nodded, getting to his feet as the last bit of blackness dripped from his naked, bloody body. Scrapes and glass freckled his face and shoulders, and his left eye was swollen shut. Great patches of his hair and eyebrows were missing, having been burned off. His brain felt like it was boiling inside his skull, and he couldn't breathe. "Let's finish this, bitch. If you think you got what it takes."

All at once, he couldn't hear anything anymore. The flames around him started to dance and scatter away, until they were snuffed out completely. Xander looked around in confusion as a wind came from nowhere, swirling about with the force of a tornado. Zakron looked even more confused, batting debris that swirled around it as if they were its enemy. The sound like a rhythmic beating filled the air, as Xander recognized it, looking upwards just in time to see the clouds part, and a huge military helicopter descend from the sky. It hovered about twenty feet above the ground, and three cords came out of a hole in its underside. Three men, all of them wearing what resembled forest green scuba gear, slid down the ropes and landed gracefully on the ground. All three opened fire at Zakron, shooting darts into the demon's backside, and it went down in a slump. After nearly a half hour of battling it, Xander watched the thing go down with three darts.

"Obtain! Obtain!" yelled the lead scuba-man. There were yellow stripes on the side of his right arm. They all wore air tanks and dark goggles, showing none of their skin. They were muscular, but human in their movements and mannerisms.

"Hey!" Xander yelled, running up to the leader. "What the hell is going on here?"

"Classified, son," the commander nodded, putting an arm on Xander's shoulder. "Circe business. None of your concern. Thanks for keeping him in one place long enough for us to get a bead on him, though," he said gratefully, turning away to grab the rope and climb up as the other two loaded Zakron into the chopper.

"Hey!" Xander yelled again, grabbing the man by the arm and pulling him back down to earth. "Where do you think you're going? I've got a lot of questions, and I know you've got answers!"

"Sorry, kid," the man shrugged honestly, turning and firing a dart into Xander's gut. "Classified."

Xander fell to the ground, remaining there for a moment, unable to move. He was only able to watch the chopper pull back into the clouds and away from sight.

As soon as he could move again, he ran into the penitentiary and grabbed up the body of Adam Genblade, taking off for the nearest hospital.

CHAPTER TEN:
FATHERHOOD

Xander watched, wrapped up in a blanket he'd been handed by a nurse as the doctors removed the last few slivers of pipe from Genblade's side.

He was in a coma, they said.

Extensive head trauma, his skull had been crushed. They said there was so much brain damage the man had little to no hope of ever waking up again. They said it was a fitting punishment, living death like that. He hadn't formed an opinion yet.

Shaking his head, he turned and walked into the next room where Cathy lay weakened on her hospital bed, as Mike spoon-fed her oddly colored Jell-O.

"The doctor says you should try to eat," Mike reminded her for the fifth time as she refused to so much as open her eyes, let alone her mouth.

"If the doctor says eat, then eat, Cat," Xander said flatly, trying not to show what he was feeling. Trying not to break down and cry. She was eating for one again, but she was all right, thank God. A few cracked ribs, a twisted ankle and a sprained wrist, but all things considered, they said she got off lucky.

They obviously never looked up the definition of the word.

The force of Zakron's throw had killed the young life inside her. Tears ran down her cheeks as she refused to eat, refused to move. She just sat there, clutching her gut, her face turning colors as the grief overcame her. Her mother and sister came in and told the boys to leave. They did.

Outside, Mike collapsed into Xander's arms as his spirit died, along with all the hopes and dreams of a young father.

EPILOGUE

THURSDAY, DAY TWENTY-THREE

The five of them sat in silence, nobody sure of what to say or how to react.

Cathy still sat in her hospital bed, her pillow soaked with tears and her sheets tinged with the blood of her child that was still leaking its way out from between her legs. She twitched. She hadn't spoken a word since it had happened, not even to her own mother. Her sister had yelled at her for overreacting, saying she should be glad to be rid of it anyway, that she should be thankful. Thankful that her child was dead before it had even gotten a chance to live, that she had nothing to remember it by, not even a picture or an ultrasound, nothing. In the last four months, Cathy had been raped, beaten, molested, assaulted, and tortured. But this was the first time, she thought, she'd ever known real pain.

Mike sat next to her, his hands laying on the bed, waiting for the moment when she would take them. When she would turn to him for comfort and love. The moment did not come, instead all he got were cool stares that put him in his place every few moments, that let him know where he stood and made him feel the same way she did inside. It was like his guts were about to turn over, and every second he was trying to stop himself from throwing up. All he wanted to do was cry, but he couldn't. He had to be strong – he had to fight this.

Julie was on Cathy's other side, stroking her hair soothingly, surprisingly silent. She knew that nothing she could say would make it better, nothing would take the pain away. She turned to look at Xander every few seconds, brooding in the corner, shooting him a pitiful smile. They both knew it was fake, its only purpose to try and get him to reciprocate it, which he never did.

Mandy sat in a chair and tried not to get noticed, her hood pulled over her head until it was almost invisible.

Why is it that no matter what happens, no matter how much good is done, there's always something horrible waiting to beat it down? Xander wondered, as he leaned against the corner, his arms crossed against his chest. *Cathy had just fought her way back from the abyss that Grendel and Phillips and the rest of them had tried to plunge her into. She'd just made herself strong, taken her first steps into her real life, her first love... only to have her feet kicked out from beneath her, by something that hurt her because my scent was on her. Four Tees are dead, a girl, thirteen civilians, and one unborn child. That brings the death toll for one event to nineteen. Personally, I don't want to stick around for round two. I'm sick of it.*

Is that the lesson? That no matter how hard I try to do good, it'll be those I love the most who pay the price? Sara died because I couldn't save her. I loved her more than anything, more than I ever will love anything again. I can still feel her touch, hear her laugh... and I can see so much of her in Julie. Is this the life that I'm promising her? Death, mayhem and destruction? Pain? When ghosts of the past can't even stay buried long enough to forget them, and only the pain remains to keep you warm at night?

I thought this part of it was over. I thought things were getting better. But now, Cathy and Mike have been hurt more than Sara or Julie ever could be. Their child is gone, and it's my fault, he thought, tears welling up in his eyes. *It's all-*

"...Mike's fault," he heard Mandy mumble, almost too low for even him to hear, with his enhanced sense of hearing.

Xander raised an eyebrow, stepping over to the girl discreetly. He scratched his head for a moment, then stroked his chin. "What was that?" he whispered, touching her gently on the shoulder.

She turned to him, frowning. "Nothing."

He smiled, giving her a playful tap on the cheek. "Come on, you can tell me."

She shook her head, shooting him an annoyed look. "It's all Mike's fault," she grumbled, glaring at the blond man weeping at his lover's feet.

Xander almost laughed, although it wasn't funny at all. "And how did you reach that conclusion?"

"That thing was after him. It wanted him, and it hurt Cathy to get to him. If Mike had just been normal, none of this would have happened."

"What are you talking about?"

She scoffed at him, curling her lip in disgust. "Don't play dumb with me," she accused, slapping him, "I know Mike's the Black Angel thing. I saw it."

Now, Xander did laugh, lightly. "I can tell you this,

Mandy, Mike is not that Black monster."

"Yes he is!" she protested, a little too loud, through gritted teeth. "I saw it! I'm sure!"

There was a knock at the door and Xander sighed, getting up from his conversation with the girl to answer it.

"Hey," Tommy said, greeting Xander with a nod as he held up a bouquet of flowers. "I know you guys probably wanna be alone with her, so I figured I'd just drop these..."

"Come in, Tom," Xander smiled, opening the door and patting him on the back as he walked past.

Cathy looked up, seeing the arrangement of roses and daisies, two of her favorites. She still didn't speak, but for the first time in days, she smiled. The grin brought tears to Julie's eyes, and she turned and walked outside the room, feeling that nobody needed to see her break down.

Xander followed her, shutting the door behind them. Julie sat on the floor, her back against the wall, her eyes red and puffy.

"They all must think I'm so stupid," she sniffed, wiping her nose in her sleeve. "Cathy always hated me, we're not even friends, but look at me."

"Nobody thinks you're stupid," Xander sighed, sitting down next to her, his hand automatically clasping hers while his other wiped her tears away even as more came.

She sniffed hard, her body shaking from tears. "It's just hard to see anyone like that, you know? I mean, that could have been me, and I can't imagine."

"I know. Shh," he soothed, bringing her head to his shoulder and kissing the top of it lightly, stroking the side of her face.

"And then she smiled, and I couldn't take it anymore. It just means so much that she could even smile after something like that. I can barely smile thinking about it... and... mine... are... all... fake... and..." she stuttered, her throat raked with tears, then she sniffed and started again, "and when I smile it's still fake but hers was real and she's so amazing. How can she?"

He smiled, kissing her head again. "I'll never know," he responded honestly. "She's truly the strongest person I know. The best of all of us."

Julie nodded, wiping her tears in his collar. Her nostrils cleared a little, and she smelled his aftershave, smiling at the musty odor. "I get it now," she whispered to him as she calmed down.

"Hmm?" he asked, pulling her close and squeezing her, despite the pain it caused his cracked and bruised ribs. "Get what?"

"What you were talking about before. At Sara's grave, and before that thing came to the school. When you were talking about all the stuff that happened, and how you were worried about the people you love and everyone that died. I get it now, I understand. I know why you have to try and help, why you need to save everyone. It's not some stupid macho trip or anything, it's... it's Cathy's smile. When Tommy brought in those flowers, he was the hero. Because even though all that awful stuff happened to her, he made her smile. And it was the most beautiful thing I've ever seen. It was amazing."

Xander was silent for a moment, still stoking the side of her face, "Wow," he said after a moment.

"What?" she asked, jumping out of his arms a little.

"Am I wrong? If I am, I'm so sorry..."

"No," he laughed, pulling her back toward his body. "It's just... I've spent the last four months trying to figure that out, and then you go and get it right in a few sentences."

She smiled. "Well, that's the thing about talking all the time: eventually, something smart is bound to come out. It's the law of averages," she said matter-of-factly, giving him a curt nod.

"You get me more than anyone ever has and you don't even try, do you?" he asked softly as he tilted her chin up.

Her lower lip started to quiver as he drew closer. Their lips met, moist and wet as he pulled her closer to him, feeling her arms wrap around him. She tasted like raspberries.

And all of the pain, the suffering, and the sorrow that their lives had become, turned into ghosts of the past, fading away like a feather on the wind.

And they became each other's heroes.

PREVIEW

IGNORANCE
IS BLISS

PREVIEW
IGNORANCE IS BLISS

Los Angeles, California.

She slid through the inch-wide crack in the hardwood floor beneath a stone desk, the black liquid that made up her body bubbling up like boiling, frothy milk. It spread out over the floor and started to spurt up and take shape until curves formed around her hips and breasts, and a sleek, pointed chin came into view. Cute, tiny lips emerged, along with big black eyes that gleamed with childish delight.

Seconds later, Leigh Blackheart was lying in the middle of the floor. Quickly, she stretched her slender neck and peered around the corner of the desk into the long hallway beyond, found it to be vacant, then stood up.

She stretched, took a few deep breaths and wiped the sweat from her brow, then smoothed down her short black hair until it was tight to her scalp. She took a whiff of the air, curled her nose, then looked up at the sign that hung from the ceiling.

Museum of Natural History: The Past is the Way to the

Future.

"I just hope the future doesn't smell this bad," she said, her west coast accent apparent. She turned quickly, scanning the room until she found what she was looking for. In the adjacent room was a tall glass case, inside of which was a blue gem, shimmering in the bright fluorescent lights aimed at it.

Confidently, she walked out into the room and took it in, the smell of old things still following her. She bent over the glass case with an air of sexuality, knowing that she was going to be watched by middle-aged men on security tapes when the deed was done. She read the inscription and smiled coyly to herself.

"The Gem of Aberdean... well, if that isn't a mouthful."

She reached into her pocket and pulled out a glass cutter attached to a large suction cup. She stuck it carefully to the glass, slowly twirling the blade around until a circle had been cut. Softly, she removed the device and tapped the inside of the circle.

Nothing happened.

Sighing, she tapped it again, a little harder.

Again, nothing happened.

"Oh, fuck this," she huffed, reaching back an arm and punching through the glass, shattering the entire case and grabbing the gem as alarms began to sound all around her.

Closing her eyes tightly, her feet began to melt. Her face filled with anguish as the rest of her body followed, and she again disappeared into the floor.

She reemerged a moment later outside the museum,

drenched in sweat. Looking down at the brilliant blue stone in her hand, she smiled devilishly.

"So, you're what everyone's talking about?" she smiled, turning briefly back toward the museum. "Sorry guys. When I collect the five mil for this baby, I'll be sure to send you an air freshener."

Suddenly, she screamed, dropping the gem to the grass.

Her body began to shimmer and shake, blobs boiling off of her everywhere. Even her eyes became as large as dinner plates, then as small as needle-points, as she morphed uncontrollably and fell to the ground.

She turned onto her back, an action that seemed to take all of her energy, and faced her attacker.

There stood a tall, white man with dark brown hair that came down in two long streaks on either side of his face. His face was sharp, almost to the point of being tri-angular, and his mouth was small and curled up in a ho-lier-than-thou sneer. He wore a strip of cloth across his forehead, which featured a tiny green gem in its center. His eyes were a piercing cobalt blue. The strangest thing about him was his attire. Dressed in long black robes from head to toe that covered his feet and made him look like he was floating, along with patterned pieces of ribbon that twirled about his body, engraved in gold thread with runes and Egyptian symbols. He pointed a long cane at her, and energy crackled from its tip.

If this had been a hundred years ago, she would have said that he was a nobleman.

"Who the fuck are you?" she spat, still twitching, a mixture of blood and sweat seeping from her pores.

"I, am Sebastian LeGaea," he said, making it sound royal and important with his strong Scandinavian accent. "You, are Leigh Blackheart. Formerly Leigh Draco."

He pulled back a leg and kicked her. To her shock, it actually connected.

"You are an idiot. And yet... you have accomplished something I could not, the retrieval of the gem."

"How the hell did you know I was going to be here?"

He looked down at her, raising his cane. "I hired you, you twit. I hate to inform you, but the gem is worth nothing... putting it right on par with your pathetic life."

He brought the cane down against her head, causing her to black out into a dreamless slumber.

FROM THE AUTHOR

This is a very hard 'From the Author' section for me to write.

On the one hand, I love this book. From a stylistic standpoint, I consider it one of the high-water marks for the first chunk of the Coral Beach Casefiles series.

On the other hand, we go to a darker place than I ever have before. It's not a place I enjoyed spending my time, but it was where the story took me and I don't come to the blank page lightly. As an author, sometimes you have to be fearless.

Every author experiments with the lines to see how far they can push things, and all fiction is a response to the fiction and realities that came before it. I grew up in the 90s first being fascinated with -- and later disillusioned with -- movies like Jurassic Park, where children were placed in peril... but always came out safe. Once you recognize that formula, it takes all the tension out of those movies. Anyone who reads this book and thinks the intention was violence or mere shock, I assure you that wasn't the case.

The intention was to hammer home that 'nobody is safe in these stories' mentality that I *need* you to have for later stories.

Would I write this story the same way today? Probably not. But as it stands it makes you have an emotional reaction, and it is most likely the reaction that was intended, even if that reation isn't a good one.

This novel, like all my novels, is dedicated to Ellen.

Special thanks also go to the ever under-appreciated Engen editorial staff. With their help I think we've made this the best Engen Book yet, and they also helped me make some hard choices when deciding how much of this story needed to be told.

- Matthew LeDrew, author
June 15, 2019
St. John's, Newfoundland

ENGEN TIMELINE

With over twenty novels spread over three different series by many different authors, the Engen Universe of titles is growing every day and into genres we couldn't have imagined! From the original ten book *Coral Beach Casefiles* thriller series, its crime novel sequel series *Xander Drew*, our flagship adventure title *Infinity*, or single-novels like *Jacobi Street* or *light|dark*, there's something in the Engen Universe for everyone with more books by more authors on the way soon!

...But how do the events relate to one another, chronologically? While some astute readers have guessed at the potential timeline (some accurately, some not), we're going to finally set the question of the Engen Timeline to rest.

Turn the page for an up-to-date guide of the ever-widening world of Engen, featuring the works of Ellen Curtis, Andrea Hackett, Sarah Thompson, Jay Paulin, and Matthew LeDrew!

In the 10 Years Prior Black September

"Reptilia" by Matthew LeDrew
published in *light|dark*.
Danger descends on a small secluded town in the
form of a deadly virus with fantastic and terrible
side-effects. Can a small group of doctors escape
alive?

Compendium by Ellen Curtis
Three short stories forming the basis for the
Engen Universe's ties to suspense, genetic
engeneering, and the supernatural. Features the
stories "The Tourniquet Revival," "Falling into
Fire" and "At Midnight, the Dawn."

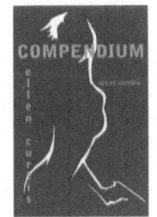

"The Theogony" by Matthew LeDrew
published in *light|dark*.
A tale of young Theo Flaherty of the *Infinity* series
and his time admitted against his will to the Black
Springs hospital, where he learns to paint, and
seeks out his father.

Black September

"Revving Engen" by Matthew LeDrew
published in *light|dark*.
A direct lead-in to both *Infinity* and *Black Womb*,
Tasha travels to Coral Beach, Maine on a hot tip
about a recently discovered young man with
incredible abilities.

Infinity by Ellen Curtis & Matthew LeDrew
Faced with a destiny he's uncertain of, the
enigmatic Victor must bring together four unique
people with very special abilities… or face the
tasks ahead alone. Guaranteed to excite!

Black Womb by Matthew LeDrew
Fifteen years ago, something happened in Coral
Beach, Maine that resulted in the present death of
a seventeen-year-old boy. Now four high-school
students must try to solve the mystery... before
the killer picks them off.

Jacobi Street by Matthew LeDrew
When a mysterious painting shows up at an art
gallery he works at, Bob must work with Eddie
and Sloan to track down its sinister origins and
convince the people living on Jacobi Street of
them, before its too late!

Transformations in Pain by Matthew LeDrew
When two girls are assaulted and one is
hospitalized, the residents of Coral Beach must
put their shared tragedies behind them and stop
the man responsible, as well as unlock the secrets
behind the true nature of the Womb...

Year One: October

Smoke and Mirrors by Matthew LeDrew
The approaching trial of Genblade brings closure
to the people of Coral Beach, until people start
showing up dead in the same manner they did
when he was at large.

"Scarlett" by Andrea Hackett
published in *light | dark*.
Introducing Scarlett, the slightly damaged hunter
on a mission to save others from the monsters
from her past.

"The Inevitable" by Ali House
published in *The Lightbulb Forest*
A young woman must contend with the
emergence of a frightening new power alongside
the emotional high of a first date.

The Tourniquet Reprisal by Curtis & LeDrew
A man lives in Atlanta, Georgia that people
don't talk about, but everyone knows he's there.
He arrived a year ago and turned a gaggle
of uneducated youth into something new,
something to fear.

Roulette by Matthew LeDrew
As the teen suicide rate in Coral Beach starts to
climb astronomically fast, Xander travels to Los
Angeles to fight his most terrifying adversary
yet… and learns that the only thing worse than
looking for release… is finding it.

Year One: November

Exodus of Angels by Curtis & LeDrew
Victor's enigmatic past is illuminated when
Jaycee accompanies him to visit a new friend
in the paliative care ward of the Black Springs
hospital, where Theo also happens to be
searching for a cure for Leigh.

Ghosts of the Past by Matthew LeDrew
Coral Beach faces its most awesome threat when
one of Engen's past mistakes is unleashed upon
the unsuspecting populous. Friends and enemies
unite to fight a common enemy… but will even
that be enough?

Touch Your Nose by Matthew LeDrew
Simon Monk must infiltrate the San Fransico branch of Shane Industries, a massive company with deep ties to the Engen Universe. Where do his true loyalties lie? And can he get out without causing harm?

Ignorance is Bliss by Matthew LeDrew
After being set through the ringer one too many times, Xander decides that his life with Julie needs a little more attention… which is bad news because a new villain has come to town with his sights set on Adam Genblade.

"Gristle While You Work" by Jay Paulin published in *light|dark*.
A short story centering around the rise of a new, and possibly cannibalistic, serial killer in the Engen Universe.

Becoming by Matthew LeDrew
For months Xander Drew has been doing his level best to keep the streets of Coral Beach clean, which means it's time for the forces of darkness to strike back… all at once.

Inner Child by Matthew LeDrew
Julie is hospitalized with life-threatening wounds to both body and soul. But the real threat comes from the hospital walls themselves, as a demonic presence makes itself known to Xander and his friends.

End of Year One

Gang War by Matthew LeDrew
The Tees, a homicidal gang of evil men, has finally been taken down by Xander Drew. But his victory is short lived, as retired Tees are mysteriously killed. With a town of suspects, anyone can be the culprit… including one of their own.

Chains by Matthew LeDrew
Sociopath Derek Smith has been freed from prison and is praying on the weak; and none are weaker than August Styles: a pregnant girl with Down Syndrome who has run away from home.

"Omega" by Ellen Curtis
published in *light | dark.*
A sinister division of Engen begins a series of experiments on pregnant women in a fashion eerily similar to those that created the original Black Womb project.

The Long Road by Matthew LeDrew
Xander meets the American people — and realizes that the world is harsh and wicked, but can also be soft and gentle, even loving. Xander Drew comes of age on the road, and sets his new direction.

Year Two

Cinders by Matthew LeDrew
Detective Horton enters a violent and dangerous world he didn't know existed beneath the veneer of order and structure that he has based his entire deductive method around.

Sinister Intent by Matthew LeDrew
One of the killers Detective Horton could not catch has resurfaced: a serial killer who flaunts his sinister intent in front of the Los Angeles Police Department, making it so that no one is safe.

Faith by Matthew LeDrew
Xander's mysterious and troublesome past returns to haunt him on the streets of Los Angeles; a place where even more people can get caught in the crossfire of the games of death and deceit that makes up his life.

Flickers in the Night by Matthew LeDrew
Lisa Rowdan is hunted by her haunting -- and powerful -- ex-boyfriend Ryan through a lonely city street. Can she escape him?
One of over twenty great sprine-tingling short stories!

Family Values by Matthew LeDrew
Xander and his new friends Crowley, Lisa, and Tim investigate a series of kidnappings and murders that stretch back decades, all of which have the same similar twist: victims being found after years of being missing.

The Future

Fate's Shadow by Matthew LeDrew
When one of Xander's old cases comes up for trial, Megan Greene returns with it. The former friends are led into conflict regarding her client's innocence. However, they put their difference aside when they both become targets of the vigilante known as Shiro Gilbert.

The Future

"Remers" by Sarah Thompson
published in *light | dark*.
In the not-too-distant future of the Engen
Universe, young athletes are the targets of a
scouting program to create the next stage of super
soldier with cybernetic enhancements.

The early years of **Xander Drew** as he struggles with the evils of his small rural hometown of Coral Beach, Maine. Cursed with the heart of the Womb and the gift of seeing the world around him for what it really is, Xander must learn the hard lessons about the nature of humanity to traverse the minefield of criminals, gangs, and abusers that stand between him and ultimate happiness -- but most of all that **sometimes it takes a monster, to catch a monster.**

"THE WRITING OF ITS GENERATION-- VISUAL, TO-THE-POINT AND IN-THE-MOMENT."

- *The Northeast Avalon Times*

The Coral Beach Casefiles series by Matthew LeDrew:

Book One: Black Womb (February 2019)
Book Two: Transformations in Pain (March 2019)
Book Three: Smoke and Mirrors (April 2019)
Book Four: Roulette (May 2019)
Book Five: Ghosts of the Past (June 2019)
Book Six: Ignorance is Bliss (July 2019)
Book Seven: Becoming (August 2019)
Book Eight: Inner Child (September 2019)
Book Nine: Gang War (October 2019)
Book Ten: Chains (November 2019)

Epilogue: The Long Road (December 2019)

For more information, please visit

www.engenbooks.com

THE XANDER DREW SERIES

Prologue: The Long Road (December 2019)

COMING SOON FROM ENGEN BOOKS:

FATE'S SHADOW

A violent past case is reopened as Xander must contend with Detective Thomas Horton, the vigilante Shadow Flame, and a returning figure from his youth in Coral Beach -- all while trying to prevent a murderer from running free. Can Xander stay the course even as his world crashes in around him?

ABOUT THE AUTHOR

Matthew LeDrew holds an Honours Degree in English from the Memorial University of Newfoundland with a minor in Anthropology, and studied Journalism at College of the North Atlantic in Stephenville, Newfoundland. He was honoured to be a jury member of the 2018 NLBA awards.

He has written twenty novels for Engen Books: the ten book *Coral Beach Casefiles* series, *The Long Road, Cinders, Sinister Intent, Faith, Family Values, Jacobi Street, Touch Your Nose, Infinity, The Tourniquet Reprisal, and Exodus of Angels* the latter three of which with co-author Ellen Curtis.

He lives in St. Johns, Newfoundland.